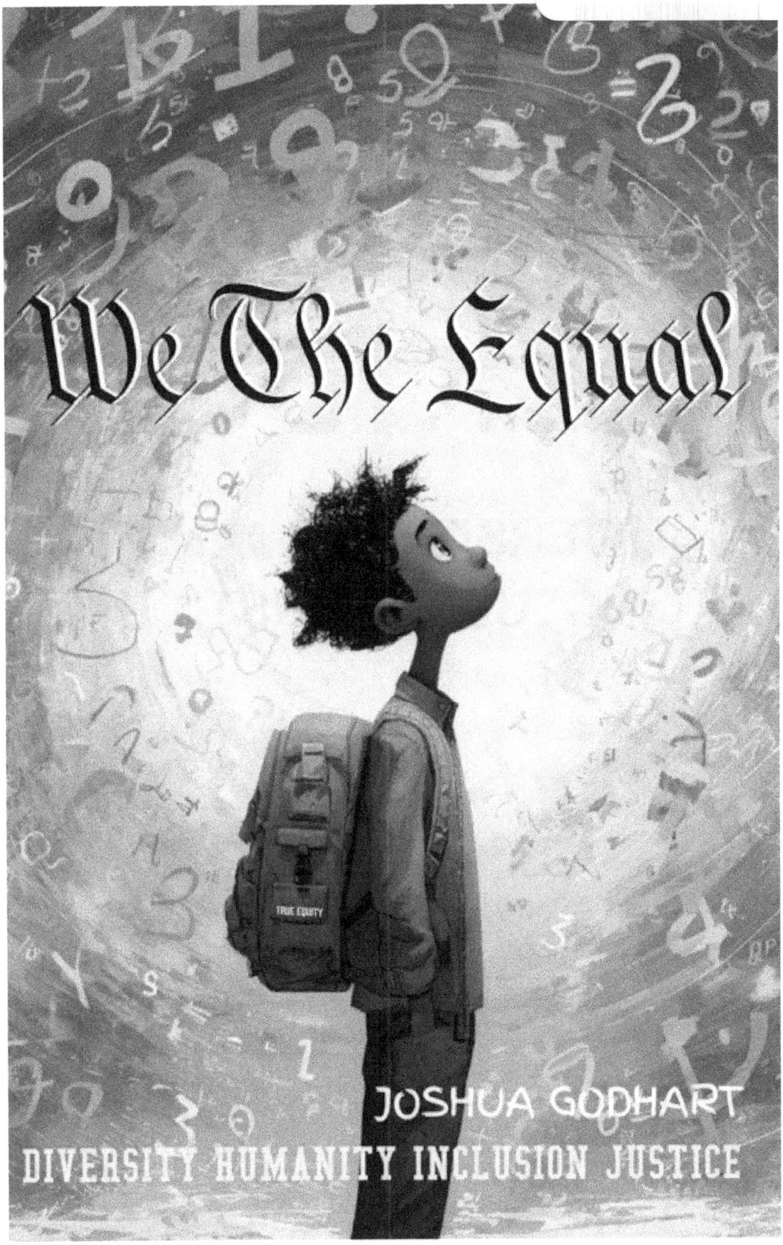
We The Equal
TRUE EQUITY
JOSHUA GODHART
DIVERSITY HUMANITY INCLUSION JUSTICE

We The Equal

DIVERSITY HUMANITY INCLUSION JUSTICE

Joshua Godhart

Distributed by Godhart Group Publishing

Brooklyn Park, MN 55443

Library of Congress Control Number: 2025919827

Table of Contents

Page intentionally left blank:

We The Equal

DIVERSITY HUMANITY INCLUSION JUSTICE

We The Equal Merchandise can be found at the following
URL: https://trueequity.creator-spring.com/

OVERVIEW

In the heart of a divided America, where the scales of justice tip unevenly and the promise of liberty rings hollow for many, young Jamal Thompson, a 12-year-old African American boy from a bustling urban neighborhood, embarks on a transformative journey. Jamal has always been captivated by the simple elegance of the mathematical equal sign (=)—a symbol that boldly declares two sides are of identical value, no matter their differences in form. But as he navigates the harsh realities of his world, he uncovers the glaring inequality that plagues his community and beyond. Through allegorical adventures in a dreamlike realm called "Equatoria," Jamal confronts the myths of American equality, drawing parallels to the Preamble of the Constitution: "We the People of the United States, in Order to form a more perfect Union..." The story weaves a tapestry of hope, revealing that true union can only be perfected when "We the People" evolves into "We the Equal"—a society where every soul is seen, valued, and empowered as inherently worthy.

This allegory is a clarion call to action, blending the innocence of childhood wonder with the fire of righteous indignation. It exposes the fractures in our nation's foundation while illuminating pathways to healing. As a passionate activist, I believe harmony isn't a distant dream but a deliberate choice: we must dismantle the barriers of prejudice, amplify marginalized voices, and rebuild with equity at the core. *We The Equal* isn't just a story—it's a blueprint for the America we deserve, where every child like Jamal can thrive without apology.

DEDICATION

To my beautiful Wife Amber who has been by my side every step of the way of my creative journey to birth 'We The Equal'. To my loving Children and Grandchildren who's wonder and promise have always inspired me and continue to inspire me. I have dreamed of a world where they all could be the best version of themselves without inequity. I continue to dream that dream for all people. If we could only embrace the timeless command to love one another…

To the Unequals—those whose voices have been silenced, whose histories erased, and whose futures stolen by the illusions of inequality. And to the youth like Jamal, Ethan, and every child awakening to the power of the equal sign: May you bridge the divides, embrace the pillars of Diversity, Humanity, Inclusion, and Justice, and forge the more perfect Union we all deserve. In loving memory of the ancestors who dreamed of equity, and in hopeful solidarity with the generations who will achieve it.

FORWARD

Hey, awesome readers! We're a big, exciting group of voices coming together to cheer you on as you dive into *We The Equal*. We're poets like Maya Angelou, who turned words into wings; leaders like Martin Luther King Jr., who dreamed big for fairness; brave fighters like Malala Yousafzai, who stands up for girls' rights; thinkers like Albert Einstein, who unlocked the universe with math; musicians like Bob Marley, who sang about unity; artists like Frida Kahlo, who painted her truth; presidents like Barack Obama, who showed hope changes things; justices like Ruth Bader Ginsburg, who battled for equal rights; and so many more, including everyday heroes who believe in making the world better. We're all here to say: You got this! This book is your adventure to build a fairer world.

Picture this: You're the hero in your own story, just like Jamal in the book. Maya Angelou once said, "It is time for parents to teach young people early on that in diversity there is beauty and there is strength." That means your unique self—your culture, ideas, and dreams—makes everything cooler and stronger, like adding superpowers to a team. No matter where you're from, you're part of the magic that makes equality real.

Martin Luther King Jr. dreamed of a day when young folks like you could play together without anyone judging skin color or background. He motivated us with, "I have a dream that my four little children will one day live in a nation where they will not be judged by the color of their skin but by the content of their character." You're making that dream come true by reading books like this and speaking up for what's right. Keep going—you're the change!

Malala Yousafzai, who fought for education even after facing danger, reminds us, "There should be no discrimination against languages people speak, skin color, or religion." You're at an age where you can stand up for friends who feel left out. Be that brave voice—inclusion starts with you saying, "Hey, let's all join in!"

Albert Einstein, the genius who loved math just like Jamal, believed, "Before God we are all equally wise - and equally foolish." That means no one's better than anyone else—we're all learning together. Use your smarts to solve problems like inequality, one equation at a time.

Bob Marley jammed about love and unity, singing lines that inspire us to fight injustice with kindness. Frida Kahlo painted her pain into powerful art, showing that your story matters. Barack Obama encouraged, "Change will not come if we wait for some other person or some other time. We are the ones we've been waiting for." You're those ones—ready to make justice happen!

Ruth Bader Ginsburg battled for women's rights, saying, "Women will only have true equality when men share with them the responsibility of bringing up the next generation." Team up with everyone to share the load. John Lewis urged, "Get in good trouble," meaning stand up for what's fair. Angela Davis fights for prison reform, Cesar Chavez for workers' rights, Marie Curie broke barriers in science, Lin-Manuel Miranda raps about history's heroes, and Serena Williams smashes stereotypes on and off the court.

Together, we say: Embrace diversity like a rainbow—it's beautiful! Show humanity by being kind. Practice inclusion by inviting everyone. Demand justice because it's right. *We The Equal* is your guide—read it, live it, and change the world. You've got the power!

—Your Chorus of Inspirers

We The Equal Merchandise can be found at the following URL: https://trueequity.creator-spring.com/

LEGAL COPYRIGHT WARNING

Library of Congress Cataloging-in-Publication Data has been applied for.

CHAPTER 1: THE MAGIC OF THE EQUAL SIGN

The morning sun hung low over Northside Minneapolis, casting long shadows across the cracked sidewalks of Broadway Avenue. Jamal Thompson, twelve years old and already taller than most boys his age, clutched his backpack strap with one hand while his mother, Aisha, gripped the steering wheel of their old Honda Civic with white-knuckled intensity. The radio hummed softly with the local news—something about budget cuts to public schools again—but Jamal wasn't listening. His mind was elsewhere, sketching invisible equations in the air, where numbers danced like fireflies in his imagination.

"Keep your hands where they can see 'em, baby," Aisha whispered, her voice steady but laced with the weariness of too many mornings like this. The flashing lights of the police cruiser reflected in the rearview mirror, turning the ordinary drive to school into a tightrope walk over an abyss Jamal was only beginning to understand.

He nodded, his wide brown eyes fixed on the dashboard. Why now? They weren't speeding. The taillight wasn't out—Aisha checked it every week. But here they were, pulled over two blocks from Jefferson Elementary, the siren a brief wail that echoed through the neighborhood like a warning bell. Jamal's heart thudded in his chest, not from fear exactly, but from the puzzle of it all. It didn't add up.

The officer approached, his boots crunching on the gravel shoulder. A white man with a mustache that looked like it belonged in an old Western movie. He tapped on the window, and Aisha rolled it down with a polite smile that didn't reach her eyes.

"License and registration, ma'am."

"Of course, officer." Aisha moved slowly, deliberately, pulling the documents from the glove compartment. Jamal watched, his mind racing. In math, things were simple: 2 + 2 = 4. Always. No questions, no exceptions. But here, in the real world, the rules seemed bent, like a ruler warped by heat. Why did this happen more to them than to the families in the suburbs he'd seen on TV?

The officer scanned the papers, his gaze flicking to Jamal in the passenger seat. "Heading to school?"

"Yes, sir," Aisha replied. "My son's in sixth grade."

The man nodded, but his eyes lingered a second too long on Jamal's faded hoodie, the one with the hole in the sleeve from last winter's playground scuffle. "Alright, just a routine stop. Drive safe."

As they pulled away, Aisha let out a breath she seemed to have been holding since birth. "You okay, Jamal?"

"Yeah, Mama." But he wasn't. Not really. It was the third time this year. His friend Marcus said it was because they were "driving while Black," a phrase Jamal had heard whispered in the barbershop but didn't fully grasp. It felt like an unsolved equation, variables missing, the equal sign mocking him from afar.

By the time they reached the school parking lot, the incident had faded into the background hum of daily life, like the distant rumble of the light rail. Jefferson Elementary squatted on a patch of asphalt surrounded by chain-link fences, its brick facade chipped and weary under the Minnesota sky. The building was a relic from the 1960s, underfunded and overcrowded, with classrooms where the heat worked sporadically and the textbooks were older than Aisha. Jamal hopped out, slinging his backpack over one shoulder.

"Love you, baby. Learn something good today."

"Love you too, Mama." He waved as she drove off to her shift at the hospital, where she scrubbed floors and changed linens for twelve hours a day, dreaming of the nursing degree she'd never quite finished.

Inside, the hallways buzzed with the chaos of morning arrivals—kids shouting in Somali, Spanish, and English, a tapestry of voices that made Jamal feel both at home and adrift. Northside was diverse, a word his social studies teacher threw around like confetti, but Jamal saw it as a giant math problem: so many different numbers, all trying to find their place on the number line. He slipped into Ms. Patel's math class just as the bell rang, taking his seat in the back row where the desk wobbled on uneven legs.

Ms. Patel, a kind woman with glasses perched on the end of her nose and a sari peeking from under her cardigan, clapped her hands for attention. "Alright, class, today we're diving deeper into equations. Remember, an equation is a statement that two things are equal. Like this: $x + 3 = 7$. What does the equal sign tell us?"

Hands shot up, but Jamal's mind was already whirring. The equal sign. It was his favorite symbol, a pair of parallel lines that declared fairness with unyielding certainty. In his notebook, he doodled it obsessively—bridges connecting islands of numbers, ladders reaching toward infinity. To Jamal, it wasn't just math; it was magic. It promised that no matter how different the left side looked from the right—fractions tangled with decimals, variables hiding secrets—they could balance. They could be the same.

"Jamal? Care to share?"

He blinked, realizing the class was staring. "Uh, it means they're worth the same. Like, no matter what, they're equal."

Ms. Patel smiled. "Exactly. The equal sign is the great equalizer. It doesn't care about appearances; it cares about value."

Value. The word stuck in Jamal's throat like a piece of candy gone wrong. In class, they solved for x, isolating variables until everything made sense. But outside these walls? He thought of the police stop, of how his mama's value seemed to shrink under that officer's gaze. Was there an equal sign for people?

The lesson continued, with worksheets passed out on balancing equations. Jamal flew through his, his pencil a blur. $4x - 2 = 10$. Add 2 to both sides: $4x = 12$. Divide by 4: $x = 3$. Perfect. Balanced. But as he worked, he noticed the kid next to him, Sofia, struggling with her page. She was new, from Guatemala, her English halting but her eyes bright.

"Need help?" Jamal whispered.

She nodded, pointing to a problem: $2(y + 1) = 8$.

"Distribute the 2 first," he said, sketching it out. "$2y + 2 = 8$. Subtract 2: $2y = 6$. Divide: $y = 3$."

Her face lit up. "Thanks, Jamal. You're good at this."

He shrugged, but inside, a warmth spread. Helping felt like drawing an equal sign between them—her confusion and his clarity balancing out.

Recess brought the usual scramble to the playground, a patch of cracked blacktop with rusted swings and a basketball hoop missing its net. Jamal joined a pickup game with Marcus and a few others, the ball thumping against the ground like a heartbeat. But even here, the imbalances crept in. The school across town, in the whiter suburbs, had turf fields and shiny equipment—Jamal had seen pictures online. Why not here? It was like the funding equation was rigged: rich neighborhoods + taxes = better schools. Poor ones like Northside? Left with the scraps.

As the game wound down, Jamal spotted Ms. Harmony across the yard. She wasn't a teacher; she ran the after-school program at the community center down the block, a haven of books, art supplies, and hot meals for kids whose parents worked late. Gray-haired and sharp-eyed, with a laugh that could fill a room, Ms. Harmony was a legend in Northside. Folks said she'd marched with Dr. King back in the day, her stories weaving history into life lessons.

"Hey, young scholar," she called, waving him over. "How's that brain of yours today?"

"Full of equals," Jamal said, grinning.

She chuckled. "Equals, huh? That's a powerful word. You know, in math and in life."

He nodded, but something in her tone made him pause. "Ms. Harmony, why doesn't everything balance like in equations?"

Her eyes softened, the lines around them deepening like rivers carved by time. "Ah, child, that's the question, isn't it? The world's full of promise keepers and promise breakers. But you keep asking. That's how change starts."

The bell rang, pulling him back to class, but her words lingered. Afternoon lessons blurred—reading about the Constitution in social studies, where the teacher droned on about "We the People" and a "more perfect Union." Jamal traced the words in his textbook, wondering who "We" really included. The Founding Fathers, with their wigs and quill pens, seemed so far away, their ideals lofty but distant, like stars in a polluted sky.

After school, Jamal walked the three blocks home, the autumn wind whipping leaves around his ankles. The neighborhood was alive: Mr. Lopez's food truck dishing out tacos, kids on bikes weaving through traffic, the mural on the corner store depicting hands of all colors clasped together. Diversity, his teacher called it. To Jamal, it was the raw material for a grand equation, all these different terms waiting to be balanced.

Home was a second-floor apartment in a brick building that groaned like an old man. Aisha wasn't back yet, so Jamal let himself in with the key around his neck. The place was small but warm, filled with the scent of last night's collard greens. He dropped his backpack and headed to the kitchen table, pulling out his notebook.

Doodles spilled across the pages: equal signs as swords, as chains broken free, as bridges over chasms. He imagined a world where people were like numbers—each unique but equally valuable. No one left out, no one diminished. But reality intruded. The eviction notice taped to the fridge from last month, when Aisha had worked double shifts to catch up on rent. The news clipping she'd saved about George Floyd, just a few miles away, a reminder that lives could be equations solved too soon.

As the sun dipped lower, casting golden light through the window, Jamal's thoughts turned inward. What if the equal sign was a lie? In math, it worked. But in America, for kids like him—Black, poor, from the "wrong" side of town—it felt like a trick. He closed his eyes, exhaustion from the day pulling him under, and in that twilight between wake and sleep, a strange vision flickered.

He saw a land of living numbers, where equations walked and talked, but something was wrong. The equal signs were twisted, bent into walls that separated the strong from the weak. A shadowy figure laughed in the distance, his voice like thunder: "Equality? Only for some."

Jamal jolted awake, heart racing. It was just a dream, he told himself. But the intrigue lingered, a puzzle begging to be solved. Little did he know, the portal to Equatoria was cracking open, ready to pull him into a world where math and justice collided.

Aisha arrived home as dusk fell, her scrubs rumpled, a bag of groceries in hand. "Hey, baby. How was school?"

"Good," Jamal said, helping unpack. "Learned about equations."

She smiled, ruffling his hair. "My little mathematician. You know, your grandma used to say math is the language of the universe. Fair and true."

"But what if it's not fair here?" he blurted, the words tumbling out.

Aisha paused, setting down a can of beans. "What do you mean?"

"Like today, with the cop. Or school being all messed up. It's like the equal sign doesn't work for us."

Her face softened, and she pulled him into a hug. "Oh, Jamal. It's complicated. But people are fighting to make it right. Like Ms. Harmony says, we build the bridges ourselves."

That night, as Jamal lay in bed, the city's sounds filtering through the thin walls—sirens, laughter, arguments—he pondered the Preamble they'd read in class. "We the People... to form a more perfect Union." Perfect? It felt imperfect, cracked like the sidewalks outside. Without diversity making it strong, humanity binding it, inclusion inviting all, and justice balancing it, how could it stand?

The question echoed in his mind, a seed of intrigue planting itself deep. Tomorrow, perhaps, he'd ask Ms. Harmony more. For now, sleep claimed him, and in his dreams, the equal sign glowed, calling him to a greater adventure.

But in the heart of Northside, where hopes clashed with harsh truths, Jamal's journey was just beginning. The magic of the equal sign was real, but so were the forces arrayed against it. And as the moon rose over Minneapolis, whispering promises of change, one boy dared to believe he could rewrite the equation.

CHAPTER 2: CRACKS IN THE EQUATION

Jamal Thompson kicked a pebble along the cracked sidewalk of Plymouth Avenue, the heart of Northside Minneapolis, where the air always carried a mix of barbecue smoke from corner grills and the faint, acrid tang of exhaust from passing buses. It was a Thursday afternoon in early fall, the kind where the sun hung low and golden, painting the murals on brick walls with a deceptive warmth. At twelve, Jamal was already tall for his age, his lanky frame bundled in a faded hoodie that read "Mathlete in Training." In his backpack, alongside his notebook filled with doodled equal signs—those perfect bridges connecting numbers like 2+2=4 or x=y—he carried the weight of questions that no equation could solve.

He was heading home from school with his best friend, Malik, who lived two blocks over in a row of shotgun houses that had seen better days. Malik was chattering about the latest video game, his voice rising with excitement. "Man, you gotta see this level—it's like solving puzzles but with lasers!" Jamal nodded, half-listening, his mind still replaying the math class where Ms. Patel had praised his quick grasp of algebra. "You're a natural, Jamal," she'd said. "Equality in math is pure—it's fair." Fair. The word echoed in his head like a promise.

But as they turned the corner onto Emerson Avenue, the world shattered that illusion. A police cruiser idled at the curb, its lights flashing silently like predator eyes in the dusk. Two officers, both white, stood over a Black teenager Jamal recognized from the neighborhood—Darius, a high schooler who worked part-time at the corner store. Darius's hands were up, his backpack slung open on the ground, contents spilling out: textbooks, a water bottle, a crumpled bag of chips. One officer was patting him down, the other shining a flashlight in his face despite the lingering daylight.

"What'd he do?" Malik whispered, freezing in place. Jamal's stomach twisted. Darius hadn't done anything—they all knew that. He was just walking home, same as them. But in Northside, walking while Black was enough to draw suspicion. Jamal had heard the stories from his mom, whispered warnings about "driving while Black" or "existing while Black." The Department of Justice report from a couple years back, after George Floyd's murder right here in Minneapolis, had blasted the police for stopping Black folks over six times more than whites. It was in the news, in the air, a statistic that felt like a scar on the city's soul.

"Hey, kid, keep moving," one officer barked at them without looking up. Malik tugged Jamal's sleeve, but Jamal couldn't tear his eyes away. Darius's face was a mask of resigned anger, his voice steady but edged. "I ain't got nothing, officer. Just heading home." The search continued, invasive, unnecessary. Jamal's fists clenched. Why? Why did the math of this place always add up wrong? In school, 1=1 no matter what. But here, Black lives seemed to equal less—less safety, less trust, less value.

They hurried past, Malik muttering under his breath. "That's messed up, J. Darius is cool; he gives us free candy sometimes." Jamal nodded, but inside, a crack formed, spiderwebbing through his love for equations. If math was fair, why wasn't life?

The unease followed him home, a shadow lengthening with the sunset. His mom, Aisha, worked double shifts at the hospital, so Jamal often stopped at the community center on Lyndale Avenue—a squat building with peeling paint and a sign that read "Northside Unity Hub." It was a haven, funded by grants that always seemed on the brink of drying up. There, amid the hum of after-school programs and the scent of fresh coffee, he found Ms. Harmony.

Ms. Harmony—everyone called her that, like she was music personified—was in her seventies, her silver hair twisted into elegant locs adorned with beads that clicked softly as she moved. She ran the center's history club, her office a cozy chaos of books, protest posters from the '60s, and a worn quilt draped over her chair. Her face was a map of life's battles: deep laugh lines around her eyes, a scar on her cheek from a long-ago march in Selma. But her smile was warm, disarming, hiding the steel beneath.

"Jamal, my young mathematician!" she called as he entered, her voice a melody of Southern drawl mixed with Midwest grit. She was sorting flyers for an anti-gentrification rally, her glasses perched on her nose. "Come in, child. You look like you've seen a ghost."

He dropped his backpack and slumped into the chair opposite her desk. "Not a ghost, Ms. H. Just… stuff." He hesitated, then spilled it: the stop with Darius, the way the officers treated him like a variable in a bad equation—something to subtract, not add.

Ms. Harmony's eyes softened, but her jaw set firm. She leaned back, folding her hands. "Ah, the cracks. They start small, but they run deep. I've seen 'em my whole life." She paused, her gentle humor surfacing. "You know, back in my day, we called it 'profiling.' Now it's got fancy reports from the Justice Department proving what we already knew: Black folks get stopped six, seven times more than whites right here in Minneapolis. It's like the system's got a bias built in, skewing the scales."

Jamal frowned. "But why? In math, if something's unequal, you balance it. Add to one side, subtract from the other. Why can't we do that here?"

She chuckled softly, but there was no mirth in it—only the echo of battles fought. "Oh, honey, if only it were that simple. See, America's got its own math problem. It started way back, with words that sound pretty but hide the rot." She reached into her desk drawer and pulled out a yellowed booklet—the U.S. Constitution. Flipping to the front, she read aloud: "'We the People of the United States, in Order to form a more perfect Union, establish Justice, insure domestic Tranquility, provide for the common defence, promote the general Welfare, and secure the Blessings of Liberty to ourselves and our Posterity…'"

Jamal listened, the words rolling like a poem. "Sounds good. Like everyone's included."

Ms. Harmony's eyes twinkled with that masked resolve. "Sounds good, but let's crack it open. When they wrote that in 1787, 'We the People' didn't mean everybody. It meant white men who owned land. Slaves like my ancestors? Counted as three-fifths of a person for taxes and representation, but no rights. Indigenous folks? Erased, their lands stolen. Women? Invisible. Immigrants? Not even a thought. It was aspirational, sure—a dream of union—but built on exclusion. Without diversity in that 'We,' it was monotonous, weak. No varied perspectives to innovate or heal."

She leaned forward, her voice dropping to a conspiratorial whisper, drawing him in like a story around a campfire. "And humanity? Absent. They dehumanized us—turned people into property, variables without souls. Inclusion? Ha! It was deliberate exclusion, creating insiders and outsiders. Justice? A foundation cracked from the start, with wrongs unaddressed, breeding resentment. How can a perfect union exist without those pillars? It can't, Jamal. Without diversity, it's uniform tyranny. Without humanity, it's cruel machinery. Without inclusion, it's alienation. Without justice, it's chaos sowing discord. The Preamble's effect evaporates—like an equation with missing terms, it never balances."

Jamal absorbed her words, feeling them settle like weights on his chest. "So, the math of America… it's rigged?"

"Exactly," she said, her humor peeking through again. "Like a test where some kids get pencils and others get stubs. But here's the hope, child: We can rewrite it. Through action—marches, votes, stories. I marched with Dr. King, felt the fire hoses, but we kept going. Small acts add up."

As she spoke, Jamal's eyes grew heavy. The room blurred, the posters of Malcolm X and Rosa Parks swirling like portals. Ms. Harmony's voice faded into a hum, and suddenly, he was falling—tumbling through a vortex of numbers and symbols, equal signs twisting like vines.

He landed softly on a ground that shimmered like graph paper, infinite lines stretching in all directions. Equatoria. The name came to him unbidden, as if whispered by the wind. Around him, equations danced alive: $5+3=8$ marched in orderly lines, but others faltered. A group of variables—x, y, z—huddled together, their forms flickering like shadows. But they weren't equal; some glowed bright, others dim, rigged by invisible forces.

"Welcome, seeker," a voice boomed, cold and sly. Jamal spun to see a figure emerging from the mist—The Divider. Tall and cloaked in swirling inequalities ($>$ and $<$ signs wrapping like chains), his face was a mask of charisma, eyes glinting with manipulative intellect. "Here in Equatoria, the math is pure… for some."

Jamal backed away. "Who are you? Where am I?"

The Divider laughed, a sound like cracking ice. "I am the keeper of balance—or imbalance, as it suits. See?" He waved a hand, and an equation appeared: White Privilege + Systemic Bias = Opportunity. But beside it, Black Resilience - Resources = Struggle. "Fair, isn't it? The strong thrive, the weak… adapt."

"No!" Jamal protested, his fiery determination sparking. "That's not equal. In real math—"

"Ah, but this is the math of your world," The Divider interrupted, his voice dripping justification. "Look around. See the dehumanized variables?"

Jamal followed his gaze. The dim variables moved mechanically, stripped of color, emotion—dehumanized, lacking humanity's bond. One, a shadowy form resembling

Darius, was pinned by greater-than signs, profiled and diminished. "They're just numbers," The Divider sneered. "No diversity to enrich, no inclusion to invite, no justice to balance. Without those, union? A joke."

Intrigue built as Jamal explored. He stumbled upon a crumbling wall of bricks labeled "Gentrification," where families—equations of homes and dreams—were evicted, their values subtracted to make way for shiny new constants. A family of variables, dark-hued like his own community, pleaded as their home equation dissolved: Rent Hike > Income = Displacement. "We've lived here for generations," one cried, but the wall grew, excluding them.

Deeper in, he found a field of unbalanced scales, justice absent. Black variables were weighed heavier with penalties, while others floated light. "Historical exclusions," a whisper explained—echoes of the Preamble's flaws. Slaves as fractions, indigenous as zeros erased.

Jamal's fear mounted—trapped in inequality, losing innocence. But then, a familiar voice: "Child, remember the pillars." Ms. Harmony appeared, ethereal, her form woven from equal signs. "Diversity strengthens, humanity connects, inclusion invites, justice corrects. Without them, this realm—and yours—crumbles."

Together, they navigated traps: A maze of binary norms excluding spectrum identities, a pit of poverty overlooking women of color. Ms. Harmony shared stories—her march on Washington, facing dogs and doubt, but uniting diverse voices. "We bridged gaps with empathy," she said, humor glinting. "Even when they called us radicals, we laughed and linked arms."

As The Divider loomed, twisting signs into barriers, Jamal solved a puzzle: Adding diversity (varied symbols), humanity (emotive glows), inclusion (open gates), justice (balanced weights). The equation shifted: We the People + Pillars = We the Equal.

But the dream cracked, pulling him back. He awoke in the center, Ms. Harmony's hand on his shoulder. "You saw it, didn't you? The cracks."
Jamal nodded, transformed. "We have to fix it."
Her smile was resolute. "Yes, we do. Starting right here, on the Northside."

CHAPTER 3: MEETING THE UNEQUALS

Jamal blinked against the shimmering haze of Equatoria, his sneakers sinking into what felt like soft, glowing graph paper that stretched endlessly under a sky dotted with floating equations. The air hummed with the faint whisper of calculations—addition signs linking arms like old friends, multiplication symbols blooming like flowers in a garden of logic. But something was off. The equal signs, those perfect bridges of balance he loved so much, were warped here. Some bent like broken spines, others stretched thin as if pulled apart by invisible hands. In the distance, grand structures rose like monuments: a towering scale tipped wildly to one side, a wall of numbers stacked unevenly, favoring the higher digits while the lowers crumbled below. He had tumbled through the dream portal Ms. Harmony had shown him, her words echoing in his mind: "The math of America isn't adding up, child. Go see for yourself." Now, here he was, twelve years old and alone in this bizarre realm, his heart pounding with a mix of wonder and unease. The real world—Northside Minneapolis, with its cracked sidewalks, the distant wail of sirens, and the warmth of his mom's kitchen—felt like a fading memory. But the injustices he'd glimpsed there, like the police lights flashing on his friend Marcus's face for no reason other than his skin, lingered like shadows.

A soft murmur drew him forward. Around a bend in the graph-paper path, where the lines curved into a hidden valley, he spotted them: a cluster of figures huddled around a flickering fire made of glowing variables. They weren't numbers or symbols exactly, but beings shaped like people, each radiating a faint aura that pulsed with stories untold.

There were six of them, diverse in form and color, yet bound by an invisible thread of shared sorrow. As Jamal approached, they turned, their eyes widening in surprise.

"Who are you?" Jamal asked, his voice echoing strangely, as if amplified by the realm's mathematical acoustics.

The group exchanged glances. One, a woman with skin like weathered earth and hair flowing like river reeds, stepped forward. She was Lila the Forgotten, though Jamal didn't know that yet. Her presence carried the weight of ancient oaks, resilient yet scarred by axes long gone.

"We are the Unequals," she said softly, her voice a poetic lilt that evoked windswept plains. "The ones left out of the equation. And you, young one? You look like you've just crossed the divide."

Jamal swallowed, glancing back at the portal's fading glow.

"I'm Jamal. From… the real world, I guess. Ms. Harmony sent me. She said I needed to see why equality doesn't work the way it should."

A murmur rippled through the group. Another figure, a man with a sturdy build and eyes sharp as border fences, nodded. This was Carlos the Bordered, his aura flickering like a candle in a storm, hopeful yet guarded.

"Ms. Harmony? She's a legend here," Carlos said with a wry smile, his accent warm like sun-baked clay. "Come, sit. We've got stories that might answer your questions. But beware—the Divider lurks nearby. He twists everything."

Jamal settled on a log-shaped logarithm, the fire's warmth chasing away the chill of uncertainty. The group introduced themselves one by one, each name unfolding like a variable in a complex formula.

"I'm Lila," the first woman said, her introspective gaze drifting to the horizon. "I represent the forgotten roots of this land—the Indigenous peoples whose histories have been erased from the grand equation." Her motivation burned quietly: to reclaim the visibility stolen by centuries of displacement. But fear gnawed at her—permanent oblivion, her people's legacies buried under layers of rewritten narratives.

Next was Carlos. "Carlos here. I stand for the immigrants, especially us Latinx folk, trapped behind borders that weren't always there." Resourceful and witty, he hid his determination behind optimism, driven to prove that diverse origins strengthened the whole. His deepest fear? Rejection, the endless limbo of never belonging.

Then Alex the Spectrum shimmered into focus, their form fluid, shifting colors like a rainbow defying the storm. "Alex. For the LGBTQ+ souls marginalized by rigid binaries." Vibrant and empathetic, Alex fiercely protected authenticity, motivated to expand liberty's blessings to all expressions of self. Invisibility terrified them—the erasure of their true colors in a judgmental world.

Elara the Overlooked followed, her shadow-like presence laboring even in stillness. "Elara, symbolizing women of color in poverty, the intersecting chains of gender, race, and class." Tenacious and compassionate, she defied sidelining with sharp intellect, driven to demand equity for unseen labors. Perpetual exploitation haunted her—efforts stolen without reward.

Theo the Shackled sat brooding, his chains metaphorical yet clinking faintly. "Theo. For the formerly incarcerated, especially African Americans caught in the cycle." Reflective with a hint of humor, he sought redemption through restorative justice, redefining value beyond mistakes. Relapse into rejection scared him most—eternal entrapment.

Finally, Nia the Echo, her voice resonant despite her ethereal form. "Nia, echoing the disabled communities' unheard needs." Insightful and adaptive, she amplified others, motivated to make "We the People" universal. Dismissal as a burden isolated her deepest fear.

As the fire crackled, Lila began the sharing, her story weaving allegory with history. "Long ago, in the real world's equation, my people were the original variables—the

Indigenous nations stewarding the land. But colonizers arrived, declaring the equation theirs alone. They forced us on trails of tears, like the Cherokee in 1838, marching thousands to death under the Indian Removal Act." In Equatoria's vision, she painted a scene: equal signs morphing into chains, dragging symbols across a fractured grid, lands redistributed to "greater" numbers while hers faded into shadows. "Without Diversity," she whispered, "history repeats in monochrome, stifling the mosaic that could innovate our union."

Jamal's eyes widened. He thought of school lessons glossed over, the Native names on maps without the pain behind them. "That's… that's like redlining, right? Keeping people out."

Elara nodded, her quiet defiance sharpening. "Exactly. Redlining in the 1930s—government maps coloring Black and Brown neighborhoods red, denying loans, trapping us in poverty. For women like me, it's double: wage gaps where we earn cents on the dollar, our labors in homes and fields overlooked." Her allegory unfolded: In Equatoria, she toiled in the underbelly, stacking bricks for a tower that benefited only the top, her contributions erased from the final sum. "Without Inclusion, the 'We' excludes us, perpetuating marginalization. How can a union stand when voices like mine shape nothing?"

The group leaned in, the fire reflecting their faces—a tapestry of hues and forms. Carlos chuckled bitterly. "Borders. Artificial lines drawn to divide. Think of Operation Wetback in 1954, deporting over a million Mexican Americans, many citizens, in brutal roundups. Or today's walls, separating families." In his tale, Equatoria's wall rose, a barrier of unequal symbols, trapping hopeful variables on one side while opportunities flourished on the other. "My fear? Never crossing. But contributions from all origins strengthen us. Without Humanity, we're just numbers, not people with dreams."

Alex shifted, their form rippling. "And binaries—forcing us into boxes. The Stonewall Riots in 1969, when queer folk fought back against raids, sparking pride. Yet discrimination lingers, in jobs, in laws." Their story shimmered: Equal signs snapping into rigid plus/minus, erasing the spectrum's fluidity, forcing conformity. "Invisibility crushes authenticity. Without Justice, wrongs like conversion therapy persist, mocking liberty's blessings."

Theo's brooding intensity deepened. "Mass incarceration—the new Jim Crow. The War on Drugs in the '80s, crack cocaine sentences 100 times harsher than powder, targeting Black communities. By 2008, over 2.3 million behind bars, disproportionately us." His allegory clanked: Chains of recidivism binding symbols, past mistakes defining value forever. "I seek second chances through restorative justice. But societal rejection? It traps us eternally. Without equity, the scales tip, breeding resentment."

Nia echoed softly, her voice amplifying the group's. "Disability—ugly laws in the 1800s banning 'unsightly' people from streets, institutionalization until the ADA in 1990. Yet accessibility lags." Her tale resonated: Unheard echoes in Equatoria's voids, needs dismissed as burdens. "We amplify all, but isolation in an ableist world? It silences us. Without these pillars—Diversity, Humanity, Inclusion, Justice—the Preamble's union evaporates, leaving hollow aspirations."

Jamal absorbed their words, each story a puzzle piece clicking into his mind's equation. The illusions of school math shattered; equality wasn't innate—it was fought for, often denied. "So, the equal sign… it's supposed to balance, but here, it's twisted. In America too?"

Lila nodded. "Precisely. Voter suppression ties it all—poll taxes, literacy tests post-Emancipation, modern ID laws targeting minorities. In 2013, Shelby County v. Holder gutted the Voting Rights Act, unleashing barriers."

As they spoke, a chill wind stirred. The fire dimmed, shadows lengthening. From the valley's edge emerged The Divider—a towering figure cloaked in charcoal mist, his form a sly amalgamation of sharp angles and deceptive curves. Charismatic yet cold, he exuded an intellect that twisted logic like pretzels. His eyes gleamed with manipulative glee, motivated to perpetuate superiority myths, fearing only the unity that could expose his fragility.

"Ah, the Unequals and their new pet," he sneered, his voice a velvet blade. "Spreading tales of woe? How quaint."

Jamal stood, fiery determination igniting. "Who are you?"

"The Divider, guardian of order." He waved a hand, and equal signs nearby warped into barriers, slicing the graph paper into segregated zones. "Equality? A myth for the weak. 'We the People' was never for you lot—slaves, savages, deviants." He circled, whispering poisons: to Lila, "Your lands were forfeit to progress"; to Carlos, "Borders protect purity"; to Alex, "Binaries maintain harmony."

The group recoiled, but intrigue built. The Divider hinted at a greater scheme—a hidden calculus where Preamble Guardians slumbered, flawed architects like Jefferson, whose hypocrisy he exploited. "They wrote the words, but I enforce the exclusions. Without me, chaos—diversity unchecked, humanity indulged."

Jamal's analytical mind raced. "But without Diversity, we're weak! Without Humanity, cruel! Inclusion and Justice—they're the lifeblood!"

The Divider laughed, summoning illusions: monochromatic unions crumbling, dehumanized variables marching mechanically. "See? The Preamble falters without my order. Join me, boy, or remain unequal."

Tension peaked as the Unequals rallied, their auras linking like an emerging equation. Lila's poetic insight pierced: "He's fragile—unity dismantles him."

In a surge, they pushed back, equal signs straightening momentarily. But The Divider retreated into shadows, promising return. "This is just the beginning. The trial awaits." Jamal's heart thrummed with intrigue—the Guardians? A trial? His journey deepened, the math of America unraveling into a quest for true balance.

As the fire reignited, the group bonded, their stories forging alliance. Jamal realized: hope through action started here, in empathy's embrace. Yet shadows lingered, whispering of battles ahead.

CHAPTER 4: THE PREAMBLE'S SHADOW

Jamal's footsteps echoed through the misty corridors of Equatoria like whispers in a forgotten library. The air hummed with the faint vibration of unbalanced equations, numbers flickering in the ether like fireflies trapped in a storm. He clutched the small notebook in his pocket, the one where he'd scribbled his first equal signs back in math class—simple bridges between worlds that now felt like crumbling bridges over chasms. Behind him trailed the Unequals, a ragtag assembly of souls he'd only just met but already felt bound to: Lila the Forgotten, her eyes like ancient rivers carving through stone; Carlos the Bordered, his wit a shield against the invisible walls that hemmed him in; Alex the Spectrum, shifting colors with every emotion; Elara the Overlooked, her steps silent but her presence a thunderclap of unspoken toil; Theo the Shackled, chains rattling faintly even in freedom; and Nia the Echo, her voice a resonant wave that amplified the group's quiet fears. They had escaped The Divider's initial snare in the shadowed groves of Chapter 3's meeting ground, where twisted equal signs had morphed into barbed wire fences. But Equatoria was no ordinary dream—it pulsed with the heartbeat of America's unfinished symphony, each path a vein leading to the core of its contradictions. "We have to keep moving," Jamal urged, his voice steadier than he felt. At twelve, he was the youngest among them, yet his curiosity burned like a torch in the gloom. "Ms. Harmony said the Preamble is the key. If 'We the People' is the start of the equation, then where's the equal sign that makes it balance?"

Lila nodded, her braided hair swaying like willow branches. "The ancestors whisper of shadows where the founders hide. They built the foundation on stolen earth, and now their ghosts guard the cracks." Her words carried the weight of erased histories, Indigenous lands mapped over with foreign grids. Carlos chuckled bitterly, adjusting the invisible backpack of his immigrant dreams. "Yeah, well, if they're hiding, it's because they know the math doesn't add up. Borders don't divide numbers—they divide people."

As they pressed on, the landscape shifted. The misty paths coalesced into a grand hall, its walls etched with glowing script: "We the People of the United States, in Order to form a more perfect Union..." The words looped infinitely, but gaps appeared between letters, voids where names and faces had been omitted. Jamal's heart raced. This was it—the Preamble's Shadow, a realm where the Constitution's aspirations cast long, distorted silhouettes. The air grew thick, charged with the static of unresolved debates.

Suddenly, three figures materialized from the fog, ethereal yet imposing, like statues come to life in a museum after dark.

The first was tall and lanky, with a quill pen tucked behind his ear and eyes that sparkled with conflicted brilliance—Jefferson the Flawed Founder. Beside him stood Washington the Reluctant, broad-shouldered and stern, his powdered wig a crown of hesitation. And rounding the trio was Madison the Architect, bespectacled and precise, clutching a sheaf of parchments like blueprints for a flawed machine. They were the Preamble Guardians, spectral echoes of the men who had penned America's origin story, now trapped in Equatoria to atone for its omissions.

"Who dares enter the Shadow?" Washington's voice boomed, echoing like cannon fire across a battlefield. His stoic facade cracked slightly, revealing the doubt that gnawed at his legacy—the land thefts that had paved the way for his victories.

Jamal stepped forward, his small frame defiant. "I'm Jamal Thompson. And these are the Unequals—the people your 'We' forgot." He gestured to his companions, each one a living testament to the gaps in the Guardians' grand design. Jefferson's eloquent brow furrowed, his idealism warring with regret. "Child, you tread on sacred ground. We crafted a union from chaos, a beacon for liberty. But even beacons cast shadows." His voice carried the hypocrisy of a man who wrote of equality while chaining others—a flaw that haunted him eternally.

Madison adjusted his spectacles, his analytical mind whirring. "The framework was meant to evolve. Compromises were necessary to bind the states. Yet here we stand, guardians of an imperfect equation."

The hall transformed around them. Marble benches rose from the floor, forming a courtroom of cosmic proportions. Scales hung from the ceiling, one side laden with golden privileges, the other sagging under chains and forgotten scrolls. The Divider lurked in the periphery, a shadowy spectator, his cold charisma feeding on the tension. "A trial," he hissed from the edges, his sly intellect twisting the air. "How quaint. Let the boy prosecute the past— it'll only prove my point: division is inevitable."

Jamal's pulse quickened. This was no ordinary court; it was an allegorical arena where math met morality. He was to prosecute America's hypocrisies, using proofs to expose the disparities. The Unequals took seats as witnesses, their stories the evidence. Ms. Harmony appeared in a swirl of mist, her nurturing presence a anchor. "Remember, Jamal," she whispered, her battle-hardened resolve shining through gentle eyes. "The Preamble promises a perfect union, but without Diversity, Humanity, Inclusion, and Justice, it's just ink on paper."

The trial began with a gong that reverberated through Equatoria's core. Jefferson presided as judge, his conflicted idealism making him both arbiter and accused. "State your case, young one. How has our vision failed?"

Jamal swallowed hard, pulling out his notebook. "In math, an equal sign means balance—value on both sides. But in America, it's an illusion. You wrote 'We the People,' but who was 'We'? Not my ancestors in chains, not Lila's people whose lands you took." He pointed to Lila, who rose with quiet strength.

"Exhibit one: Diversity as Strength," Jamal declared, sketching an equation on a floating chalkboard that materialized before him. "Diversity = Innovation + Resilience. Without it, Union = Uniformity - Growth." The board glowed, showing a mosaic of colors fading to gray. Lila spoke, her poetic insight weaving through the air like smoke from a sacred fire. "My people were the first stewards of this land, diverse in languages and traditions. But colonialism erased us, turning vibrant mosaics into monochrome maps. Without Diversity, the Preamble devolves into echo chambers, stifling the very progress it claims to promote."

Washington shifted uncomfortably, his commanding presence undermined by the fear of national collapse. "We fought for independence, but the divisions we ignored—land stolen, treaties broken—they fester still." His voice cracked, revealing the reluctance that had defined his leadership: the hero who freed a nation but not its original inhabitants.

Carlos leaned forward, his witty optimism sharpening into determination. "And borders? They're artificial lines in the equation, excluding contributions from all origins. I crossed deserts for a dream, only to find walls higher than promises. Without Inclusion, 'We' becomes 'Us vs. Them,' fracturing cohesion."

The scales tipped further, chains clanking ominously. The Divider smirked from the shadows, his manipulative charm whispering doubts. "See? Humans are wired for superiority. Why fight it?"

But Jamal pressed on, his fiery determination igniting. "Next: Humanity as the Core Bond." He drew a heart intertwined with variables. "Humanity = Dignity + Empathy. Absent it, Preamble = Hollow Decree." Alex the Spectrum stood, their form shimmering between hues, a vibrant emblem of fluid identity. "I've hidden my true colors to fit binary norms, fearing judgment. But liberty's blessings? They're for all expressions of self. Without Humanity, we dehumanize the different, eroding the 'People' we claim to unite."

Theo the Shackled nodded, his brooding intensity softened by humor. "Chains aren't just metal—they're systems that brand us beyond our mistakes. Mass incarceration shackles Black bodies disproportionately, ignoring redemption. Where's the Humanity in that?"

The courtroom hummed with energy, the Guardians exchanging glances. Madison, ever the perfectionist, scribbled notes, his hindsight tempering his drive. "Our compromises—three-fifths for slaves, no suffrage for women—were meant as stepping stones. But they became stumbling blocks."

Elara the Overlooked rose next, her tenacious compassion cutting through the air. "Inclusion as Active Practice. It's not tolerance; it's invitation. Women of color like me labor in shadows, our efforts exploited. Without Inclusion, the narrative is shaped by few, perpetuating marginalization."

Nia the Echo's voice resonated, amplifying the chorus. "And me? Dismissed as a burden in an ableist world. Equity must accommodate all abilities, or 'We the People' isn't universal."

Jamal synthesized their testimonies into a grand proof. "Now, Justice as the Foundation." He etched scales on the board: "Justice = Fairness + Redress. Lacking it, Perfect Union = Falters." Flashbacks flickered—Emancipation's half-measures, Civil Rights' unfinished marches, Black Lives Matter's cries echoing in streets. "Slavery's stain, redlining, voter suppression—these are imbalances you allowed. How can a union exist without Justice? It breeds resentment, mocking tranquility."

Jefferson leaned forward, regret etching his features. "We envisioned amendment, evolution. But our flaws—my own hypocrisy in owning slaves while decrying tyranny—cast this shadow."

The intrigue deepened as The Divider stepped into the light, his cold charisma commanding attention. "Enough fairy tales. Division is power. Unity? A myth." He waved a hand, summoning illusions: equal signs bending into hierarchies, numbers segregated by color. Jamal's fear surged—losing his innocence, failing his friends—but he countered with a theorem. "No! Look: Diversity + Humanity + Inclusion + Justice = Perfect Union. Without them, it's zero—nothing."

The Guardians conferred in whispers, the hall trembling. Washington admitted, "I ignored

divisions, fearing collapse. But silence enabled theft." Madison added, "My architecture compromised too much, fracturing the frame."

In a twist, Jefferson banged the gavel. "The prosecution rests. But the verdict? It's not ours—it's yours, Jamal. Rewrite the shadow."

As the chapter crested, Jamal realized the trial was a mirror, reflecting Equatoria's deeper intrigue: hidden chambers where more secrets lay. The Unequals rallied around him, their arcs intersecting in unity. Ms. Harmony smiled, her fear of forgotten sacrifices easing. But The Divider vanished with a laugh, hinting at greater battles.

The shadows parted slightly, revealing a path to the Weight of History. Jamal pocketed his notebook, the equal sign now a weapon. "We're not done. The equation continues."

CHAPTER 5: THE WEIGHT OF HISTORY

The air in Equatoria grew thicker as Jamal and his newfound companions pressed onward from the shadowed courtroom where the Preamble Guardians had laid bare their flawed legacies. The ethereal spirits—Jefferson with his eloquent regrets, Washington stoic yet doubting, Madison ever the strategist—had faded into wisps of parchment smoke, leaving behind a lingering challenge: "To perfect the Union, you must climb beyond the shadows of what was, to see what could be." Their words echoed like unsolved equations in Jamal's mind, variables dangling unresolved.

Ms. Harmony, her silver hair catching the dream-realm's shifting light like threads of forgotten wisdom, pointed toward the horizon. There, rising like a colossal imbalance in the landscape, stood the Mountain of Unbalanced Scales. Its peaks were jagged ledges of rusted iron pans, tilting precariously under invisible weights—stones of privilege on one side, feathers of forgotten lives on the other. Rivers of ink flowed down its slopes, carving canyons from erased histories, and at its base, a monochrome fog swirled, draining color from everything it touched.

"This mountain," Ms. Harmony said, her voice a steady rhythm against the wind's howl, "is the weight of history. Each step is a fight for justice, but without Diversity, it repeats in monochrome—lifeless, unchanging. Without Humanity, it crushes the soul. Without Inclusion, it leaves voices buried. And without Justice, it topples us all. Climb it, child, and feel the burden of the 'unequal people.' Only then can you bridge the gap to 'We the Equal.'"

Jamal swallowed hard, his twelve-year-old heart pounding with a mix of awe and dread. He glanced at the Unequals gathered around him: Lila the Forgotten, her form flickering like a shadow on ancient rock; Carlos the Bordered, his eyes sharp behind an invisible wall; Alex the Spectrum, shifting colors in defiance of the fog; Elara the Overlooked, her steps firm despite the shadows pulling at her hems; Theo the Shackled, chains rattling faintly with each move; and Nia the Echo, her voice resonating ahead like a guide. The Divider's presence lingered in the distance, a cold laugh carried on the breeze, but for now, they were united in purpose.

"Why me?" Jamal whispered, clutching the small equal sign pendant Ms. Harmony had given him—a talisman carved from dream-stone, glowing faintly. "I'm just a kid from Northside Minneapolis. Math class didn't prepare me for this."

Ms. Harmony's gentle humor surfaced, her eyes twinkling. "Ah, but math is life, Jamal. And life demands we solve for x—the unknown. You're the variable that can balance it all. Now, climb."

The ascent began with a deceptive ease. The path wound upward, each foothold a cracked slab etched with faded dates and names. As Jamal placed his foot on the first step, a tremor shook the ground. Visions flooded his mind, not as dreams, but as living tapestries unfolding before them all. The world around them blurred, and suddenly, they were no longer on the mountain but in a vast, frozen plain under a blood-red sky. Snow fell like ash, and in the distance, a ragged line of people trudged forward—Indigenous families, bundled in tattered blankets, their faces etched with exhaustion and grief. Horses neighed weakly, wagons creaked under meager possessions, and soldiers in blue uniforms prodded them onward with bayonets.

"This is the Trail of Tears," Lila murmured, her voice breaking the silence like a crack in stone. She stepped forward, her shadowed form solidifying, her eyes—deep pools of ancestral memory—fixed on the scene. "1830 to 1850. The Indian Removal Act, signed by President Andrew Jackson.

My people—the Cherokee, Choctaw, Seminole, and others—forced from our homelands in the Southeast. Georgia, Alabama, Mississippi—lands we'd farmed, built nations upon. But gold was found, and white settlers wanted it. So they marched us west, thousands of miles, through winter's bite and summer's fever."

Jamal watched in horror as a child, no older than himself, stumbled in the snow, her small body collapsing. A mother wailed, but a soldier yanked her forward. "How many?" he asked, his voice barely a whisper.

"Over 60,000 displaced," Lila replied, her resilient introspection giving way to quiet fury. "Thousands died—15,000 or more—from disease, starvation, exposure. They called it 'removal,' but it was genocide. Our stories erased, our languages silenced. This is the weight I carry—the fear of permanent erasure, that reconciliation will never come."

The vision intensified. The monochrome fog crept in, draining the vibrant patterns from the people's clothing, turning their diverse faces into uniform gray masks. "See?" Ms. Harmony interjected, her nurturing tone edged with resolve. "Without Diversity, history repeats in monochrome. The Preamble spoke of 'We the People,' but it excluded us—the original stewards of this land. No union can be perfect when it builds on stolen ground, ignoring the mosaic of cultures that could strengthen it."

As the vision faded, the group pressed on, the mountain steepening. Lila led now, her poetic insight guiding them around treacherous pits where forgotten treaties lay buried like landmines. "My motivation is reclamation," she confided to Jamal, her quiet strength a beacon. "To make visible what colonialism hid. But I fear the wounds won't heal if we're not included in the equation."

The next step brought a warmer haze, the air thick with Southern humidity. They stood in a cotton field under a scorching sun, where enslaved Black men, women, and children toiled, their backs bent under whips' shadows. Chains clinked like Theo's faint echoes, and overseers barked orders.

"January 1, 1863," Ms. Harmony narrated, her battle-hardened resolve shining through. "President Abraham Lincoln's Emancipation Proclamation. It declared freedom for slaves in Confederate states—but not all. The Civil War raged on, from 1861 to 1865, brother against brother, over the soul of the nation."

Jamal felt a surge of hope as Union soldiers appeared, reading the proclamation aloud. Cheers rose, tentative at first, then thunderous. But the vision shifted, revealing the aftermath: Reconstruction's brief promise shattered by Jim Crow laws. Lynchings—over 4,000 documented between 1877 and 1950—hung like dark fruits from trees. Poll taxes, literacy tests, segregation.

Theo the Shackled nodded grimly, his brooding intensity deepening. "Freedom on paper, but chains in practice. Mass incarceration's roots are here—disproportionate, endless cycles."

The monochrome fog thickened again, washing out the rich hues of African textiles and spirituals sung in the fields.

"Without Humanity," Nia echoed, her resonant voice amplifying the pain, "we're reduced to variables without souls. The Preamble's 'domestic Tranquility' rings hollow when it ignores the human cost—dehumanization eroding the 'People' it claims to protect."

Jamal's legs burned as they climbed higher. The path narrowed, forcing them single file, with avalanches of "forgotten facts" tumbling down—crumbling stones inscribed with overlooked atrocities. One nearly swept Carlos away, but Alex's fluid adaptability caught him, their shimmering form extending like a rainbow bridge.

"Watch your step," Elara warned, her tenacious compassion urging them on. "The overlooked always bear the brunt."

Another tremor: Now, the 1950s and '60s unfolded in vivid bursts. A bus in Montgomery, Alabama, 1955—Rosa Parks refusing to give up her seat, sparking a boycott led by a young Martin Luther King Jr. Then, the March on Washington, 1963, where over 250,000 gathered, King's voice booming: "I have a dream…"
Civil Rights Act of 1964, Voting Rights Act of 1965—milestones etched in gold light. But shadows crept in: Assassinations—Medgar Evers, Malcolm X, King in 1968. Bloody Sunday on Selma's bridge.
Ms. Harmony shared her own memory, her gentle humor fading into solemnity. "I was there, child. Marched with them. Felt the fire hoses' sting, the dogs' bite. We thought we'd balanced the scales, but persistent gaps remain—economic disparities, voter suppression echoing the past."
The fog descended once more, turning the diverse crowd's faces into a bland uniformity. "Without Inclusion," Carlos added, his witty optimism strained, "the 'We' excludes us still. Immigrants like my kin, bordered out, our contributions walled away. No perfect Union without deliberate invitation."
Jamal paused on a ledge, breathless. The weight pressed on him—the burden of being an 'unequal variable,' expected to carry history's load while solving for the future. "It's too much," he admitted, tears stinging. "How do I fix this? I'm scared I'll fail, lose everything—like my mom, my friends back home."
Lila placed a hand on his shoulder, her poetic insight weaving comfort. "The fear is real, but so is our resilience. Look ahead."
The final ascent brought the modern era. 2013: Trayvon Martin's death birthing Black Lives Matter, founded by Alicia Garza, Patrisse Cullors, Opal Tometi. 2014: Michael Brown in Ferguson, Eric Garner in New York—"I can't breathe." 2020: Global protests after George Floyd's murder in Minneapolis—Jamal's own city—knees on necks, streets aflame with demands for justice.

Visions of marches, chants: "No justice, no peace." But counterforces: Backlash, qualified immunity, systemic inertia. Theo laughed bitterly, his redemption-seeking humor a shield. "I'm the shackled one—formerly incarcerated, trapped in recidivism's chains. BLM fights for us, but without Justice, the scales tip forever."

As they neared the summit, the Divider's influence manifested—a storm of twisted equal signs raining down like barbed wire, trying to halt them. "You climb in vain!" his voice boomed. "Superiority is the natural order!"

But the group linked arms, their intersectional unity a shield. Nia's echo amplified their resolve, Alex's spectrum refracting the storm into harmless light.

At the peak, a vast vista unfolded: Equatoria's equations sprawling below, imbalanced but hinting at potential harmony. Yet the monochrome fog blanketed much, symbolizing repetition without change.

"How can a perfect union exist without Diversity, Humanity, Inclusion, and Justice?" Jamal pondered aloud, echoing the essential question.

Ms. Harmony answered, her nurturing wisdom a balm. "It cannot. Without Diversity, it's weak and monotonous. Without Humanity, cruel and mechanical. Without Inclusion, alienating. Without Justice, unstable. The Preamble evaporates into aspiration—slavery's stain, segregation's scars, ongoing disparities prove it. But embrace them, and 'We the People' becomes 'We the Equal.'"

Lila, transformed by the climb, stood taller. "My people's history—the Trail of Tears, Wounded Knee Massacre in 1890, where 300 Lakota were slaughtered; the 1973 occupation by the American Indian Movement demanding treaty rights—it's not just pain. It's a call to integrate our legacies into the whole."

Jamal nodded, his fiery determination igniting. The pendant glowed brighter, a promise. But as they descended, a rumble

shook the mountain—the Divider trapping the Unequals
below, forcing Jamal's choice.
The weight of history lingered, but so did hope. The climb
had revealed the fractures; now, action would mend them.

CHAPTER 6: THE BREAKING POINT

Jamal Thompson stared at the faded poster on the wall of the Northside Community Center, his fingers tracing the edges of a hand-drawn equal sign he'd sketched there during last week's after-school math club. The center was his sanctuary—a ramshackle building on Plymouth Avenue in North Minneapolis, where the air always smelled faintly of chalk dust, sweat from the basketball court, and the lingering spice of Ms. Harmony's homemade jerk chicken she brought for potlucks. It was here, amid the creaking floors and mismatched chairs, that Jamal had first fallen in love with the magic of equations. "Two plus two equals four," his teacher had said, but to Jamal, it was more: a promise that no matter how different the numbers looked, they could stand as equals.

But now, that promise felt like a lie. The letter from the city had arrived that morning, tucked into the mailbox like a venomous snake. "Due to budget reallocations," it read in cold, bureaucratic print, "funding for the Northside Community Center will be discontinued effective next month. Resources will be redirected to enhance facilities in more economically viable districts." Jamal knew what that meant—wealthier, whiter neighborhoods like Edina or Wayzata, where parks gleamed with fresh paint and community centers boasted swimming pools and tech labs. Northside, with its cracked sidewalks and boarded-up storefronts, was being erased from the equation.

He crumpled the letter in his fist, his heart pounding like a drum in his chest. The center wasn't just a building; it was where kids like him escaped the shadows of inequality. Where Ms. Harmony taught history lessons that school glossed over—the March on Washington, the Black Panthers organizing free breakfasts right here in Minneapolis. Where Carlos, the new kid from across the border, had shown up one day with a soccer ball and a grin that hid the fear in his eyes. Carlos, whose family had fled violence in Mexico, crossing deserts and rivers for a shot at the American dream, only to find it fenced off by invisible walls.

"Jamal, baby, you alright?" Ms. Harmony's voice cut through the haze, her warm hand resting on his shoulder. She was in her seventies, her silver hair twisted into neat braids, her eyes carrying the weight of Selma bridges and Freedom Rides. But today, even she looked weary, the lines on her face deeper, like cracks in a foundation too long ignored.

"It's not fair, Ms. H," Jamal whispered, his voice cracking. "They're closing us down. Like we don't matter. Like our side of the equal sign is just… less."

Ms. Harmony pulled him into a hug, her embrace smelling of lavender and resilience. "Fairness ain't given, child. It's fought for. Remember the Preamble? 'We the People, in order to form a more perfect Union…' But without justice, without including everybody—Black, Brown, immigrant, poor—it's just words on paper. A union can't be perfect if it leaves folks out in the cold."

Jamal nodded, but the anger bubbled inside him, hot and unrelenting. That night, as he lay in bed listening to the distant wail of sirens—a soundtrack to Northside life—he drifted into sleep, the letter still clutched in his hand. And as dreams claimed him, the portal to Equatoria opened once more, pulling him into its swirling vortex of numbers and symbols.

Equatoria unfolded before him like a fractured mosaic, its landscape a vast plain where equations roamed like living beasts. Giant equal signs bridged chasms, but many were twisted, bent into greater-than or less-than symbols that loomed like guillotines. The sky was a chalkboard scrawled with the Preamble's words, but they flickered erratically, words like "Justice" and "Union" fading in and out, as if the very ink of the Constitution was running dry.

Jamal landed softly on a hill of stacked variables—X's and Y's piled like forgotten rubble. His friends, the Unequals, were scattered nearby, their forms shimmering in the dreamlight. Lila the Forgotten sat cross-legged, her shadowy silhouette whispering ancient songs of stolen lands. Alex the Spectrum shifted colors like a prism, their form fluid and defiant. Elara the Overlooked hunched over, her hands calloused from invisible labors. Theo the Shackled rattled faint chains at his wrists, remnants of past bindings. Nia the Echo hovered, her voice a resonant hum that amplified the group's murmurs.

And there was Carlos the Bordered, leaning against a crumbling wall of bricks etched with words like "Deport" and "Alien." His usual witty grin was absent, replaced by a haunted expression. In the real world, Carlos was a 13-year-old with a quick laugh and a talent for soccer, but here in Equatoria, he embodied the immigrant's plight—trapped behind borders that moved like serpents, always threatening to close in.

"Jamal!" Carlos called, his voice echoing with forced cheer. "You made it back. Thought the real world swallowed you whole."

Before Jamal could respond, a shadow fell over them. The Divider emerged from a fog of distorted numbers, his form tall and imposing, cloaked in a robe of unequal signs that slithered like chains. His face was a mask of false benevolence, eyes gleaming with the cold calculus of power. "Ah, the little mathematician returns," he sneered, his voice a silky venom. "And with his band of misfits. How quaint. But tell me, boy, have you figured it out yet? Equality is an illusion for the weak. The equation of America was written by victors, for victors. 'We the People'—the right people."

Jamal's fists clenched. "You're wrong. The Preamble says 'a more perfect Union.' That means including everyone—Diversity makes us stronger, Humanity binds us, Inclusion invites us all, Justice balances the scales. Without them, it's not a union; it's a prison."

The Divider laughed, a sound like cracking glass. "Bold words from a child. But let's test your theory." With a wave of his hand, the ground trembled. Walls erupted around the Unequals—barriers of jagged inequalities, each tailored to their fears. Lila was encased in a dome of forgotten history books, pages erasing themselves. Alex was forced into a binary box, their spectrum dulled to black and white. Elara sank into shadows, her labors multiplying endlessly without reward. Theo's chains reformed, pulling him toward a pit of recidivism. Nia's echoes bounced off deaf walls, unheard and unheeded.

But the cruelest trap was for Carlos. A massive border wall surged upward, topped with razor-wire variables that spelled "ICE" and "Raid." Beyond it, a mirage of his family's home in Mexico flickered—safe but distant, a taunt of deportation. Carlos pounded against the wall, his resourceful hands searching for cracks, but it sealed tighter, whispering threats in Spanish and English: "You don't belong. Go back."

"Carlos!" Jamal shouted, rushing forward. But an invisible force held him back, the Divider's power manifesting as a gravitational pull of apathy. "This is what happens when you challenge the order," the Divider intoned. "The immigrant dreams of equality, but borders are eternal. Without Inclusion, he's forever on the outside. Without Justice, his contributions are stolen, his fears exploited. Humanity? A luxury for citizens only."

Flashbacks assaulted Jamal's mind, blending real and allegorical. He saw Carlos's story unfold like a hidden equation. In the real world, Carlos had confided in him once, during a late-night soccer game at the center. "My familia came from Jalisco," he'd said, kicking the ball with precision. "Papa worked the fields in Worthington, picking turkeys for pennies. Mama cleans houses in the suburbs. But every siren, every knock at the door—it's fear, man. Deportation hangs over us like a storm cloud. I hide it with jokes, but inside? It's like being trapped behind a wall you can't see." In Equatoria, that wall was literal. Carlos slid down it now, his hopeful facade cracking. "Jamal, it's happening again," he gasped. "In Minnesota, they say we're welcome—jobs in farms, factories. But then the raids come. Families torn apart. Kids left alone. My cousin… he was deported last year. Worked hard, paid taxes, but one traffic stop, and poof—gone. How's that justice? How's that humanity?" Jamal's heart ached. He recalled news stories he'd overheard—Latinx communities in rural Minnesota, like Willmar or Austin, where immigrants fueled the economy with backbreaking labor in meatpacking plants, yet lived in shadows of fear. Undocumented workers contributing billions in taxes, yet denied basic rights. Housing crises in the Twin Cities, where immigrant families crammed into substandard apartments, afraid to complain lest it draw attention. And now, with policies tightening, the fear amplified: schools becoming unsafe, hospitals avoided, places of worship shadowed by ICE vans.

The Divider circled, his presence a chill wind. "See? Diversity is a threat to unity. Let them in, and the equation unbalances. Humanity is for the deserving. Inclusion? Only for those who assimilate. Justice? A tool for the powerful."

But something stirred in Jamal—a fire kindled by Ms. Harmony's words, by the Preamble's flickering promise. He looked at the trapped Unequals, their faces etched with despair. Lila's eyes met his, her poetic insight whispering: "Our stories are the roots; without them, the tree falls." Alex shimmered faintly: "My spectrum lights the way—if you let it." Elara's defiance burned: "My labor built this; I deserve the harvest." Theo rattled his chains: "Second chances rewrite the past." Nia's echo amplified: "Hear us, and we all rise."

And Carlos, pressing his palm against the wall, his voice breaking: "I crossed deserts for this dream. Don't let it end here."

Jamal realized the truth: Equality wasn't natural; it was a battle. The Preamble's "perfect Union" demanded action, not apathy. Without Diversity, the nation stagnated in monochrome sameness. Without Humanity, it became a machine grinding souls. Without Inclusion, it fractured into insiders and outcasts. Without Justice, it perpetuated the very injustices it claimed to end.

With a surge of determination, Jamal broke free of the apathy field. He dashed to Carlos's wall, his hands glowing with the equal sign's light—a symbol he'd doodled a thousand times, now alive with power. "We're in this together!" he yelled. "Your story is part of ours. No more borders!"

He slammed his palm against the wall, inscribing an equal sign that burned through the bricks. Cracks spiderwebbed outward, the structure groaning. Carlos's eyes widened in hope. "Jamal, you're doing it!"

The Divider roared, summoning more barriers, but Jamal didn't stop. He moved to each Unequal, etching equals where inequalities reigned. Lila's dome shattered, her history flooding out like a river. Alex burst free, colors exploding in a rainbow defiance. Elara rose, her shadows turning to spotlights. Theo's chains melted. Nia's echoes became a chorus.

As the walls crumbled, the group converged, their combined light pushing back the Divider. He staggered, his form flickering. "You can't… this isn't the equation!"

"It is now," Jamal declared. "We the Equal—in order to form a more perfect Union."

The climax hit like a thunderclap. The Divider lashed out one final time, a wave of division crashing toward them. But Carlos, freed and fierce, grabbed Jamal's hand. "Together!" he shouted. The Unequals linked arms, a human chain of intersectionality—Black youth, Indigenous wisdom, immigrant grit, queer vibrancy, women's tenacity, reformed souls, disabled insight. The wave broke against them, dissipating into harmless mist.

The Divider shrank, his power waning. "This isn't over," he hissed, vanishing into shadows. But Equatoria trembled with change, the Preamble's words solidifying in the sky, bolstered by the pillars of Diversity, Humanity, Inclusion, Justice.

Jamal awoke with a start, the letter still in his hand. But now, resolve burned in his chest. The community center's closure was a breaking point, yes—but also a call to action. He thought of Carlos in the real world, facing real fears: the anxiety of mixed-status families, the chill of deportation raids that ripped parents from children, the economic contributions ignored amid political scapegoating.

That morning, Jamal rallied his friends at school. "We can't let them close the center," he said. "It's our fight—for equality, for us all." Ms. Harmony smiled, her eyes proud. "Lead the way, child."

As petitions circulated and voices rose, Jamal knew the journey was far from over. Equatoria's lessons echoed: Harmony demanded collective action. And in that unity, a perfect Union could finally take shape.

CHAPTER 7: ALLIES IN THE ALGEBRA

Jamal's heart pounded like a drum in a storm as he stared at the shimmering cage of twisted equal signs that encased the Unequals. The Divider's laughter echoed through the vast, equation-riddled plains of Equatoria, a sound like cracking ice over a frozen river. "See, boy? Balance is an illusion for the weak," the antagonist sneered, his form shifting like smoke, his eyes gleaming with cold calculation. The cage pulsed with dark energy, its bars morphing into inequalities—greater-than signs pointing accusingly at the trapped figures inside.

Lila the Forgotten huddled in one corner, her shadowy form flickering like a flame in the wind, whispering ancient chants of lost lands. Carlos the Bordered pressed against an invisible wall, his hands leaving faint cracks where he pushed, his witty smile strained but unyielding. Alex the Spectrum shimmered erratically, their colors—vibrant reds, blues, and purples—fading in and out, as if the cage were forcing them into a dull gray conformity. Elara the Overlooked paced like a caged panther, her eyes sharp with defiance, while Theo the Shackled rattled his lingering chains, his brooding gaze fixed on the horizon. Nia the Echo's voice resonated faintly, her words bouncing off the bars like unheard pleas in an empty hall.

Ms. Harmony stood beside Jamal, her presence a steady anchor in the chaos. "This is the breaking point, child," she said softly, her voice carrying the weight of marches long past. "But remember, equations can be rewritten. You just need the right allies."

Jamal clenched his fists, his mind racing through the math problems he'd loved back in his Northside Minneapolis classroom. In those neat notebooks, equality was simple: 2 + 2 = 4. But here, in this dreamlike realm that mirrored America's fractured soul, nothing added up. The Preamble's words—"We the People, in Order to form a more perfect Union"—rang hollow without the pillars that held it aloft: Diversity, Humanity, Inclusion, Justice. Without them, the Union was no more than a lopsided scale, tipping toward oblivion.

"I won't let this stand," Jamal declared, his voice cracking at first but growing firmer. He stepped forward, his small frame casting a long shadow in Equatoria's ethereal light. "We're not variables to be discarded. We're equals!"

The Divider chuckled, circling like a shark. "Equals? Prove it, little mathematician. Rally your ragtag band if you can. But unity? That's my greatest fear—and your impossible dream."

As if in response, a faint glow emanated from the cage. Alex's shimmering form brightened momentarily, their fluid shape rippling like water under sunlight. "Jamal," they called, their voice a harmonious blend of tones, high and low, defying any single note. "The cage… it's not just bars. It's forcing us into boxes we don't fit. But together, we can spectrum it—break the binary!"

Jamal's eyes widened. Spectrum. Of course. Alex represented the vast array of identities that America often squeezed into rigid norms, the LGBTQ+ voices marginalized by outdated binaries. Their personality—vibrant, empathetic, fiercely protective of authenticity—mirrored the fluidity of human expression. But in this cage, The Divider was stripping that away, enforcing conformity that echoed real-world discriminations: laws that erased trans rights, societies that shunned non-binary souls.

Drawing on his analytical mind, Jamal envisioned the cage as a flawed equation: Unequals < Divider. To balance it, he needed to add factors—affirmative actions, recalibrations. "Ms. Harmony, how do we rally them? How do we form coalitions?"

The elder activist smiled, her eyes twinkling with the fire of Selma and Stonewall. "By embracing Inclusion, child. It's not passive; it's an active invitation. We weave diverse threads into a stronger tapestry. Start with listening—truly hearing their stories. That's where Humanity blooms."

Jamal nodded, approaching the cage. The air hummed with tension, intrigue building like a puzzle with hidden pieces. What if the cage wasn't just a trap but a test? What secrets did the Unequals hold that could unlock it?

"Lila," he began, addressing the Forgotten first. Her introspective gaze met his, her poetic insight into land and legacy shining through. "Your people were the first variables in this equation, erased from the history books. But without your stories, the sum is incomplete. Tell me—how does Diversity heal the land?"

Lila's shadow deepened, then expanded, projecting visions of vast prairies stolen, treaties broken. "Diversity is the soil's memory," she whispered resiliently. "Without it, the Union grows barren, repeating monochrome mistakes. Include us, and we root the foundation deeper."

The cage trembled slightly, a crack forming where her words landed.

Next, Carlos. His resourceful optimism flickered as he grinned through the bars. "Amigo, borders are just lines drawn by fearful hands. My motivation? To prove immigrants like me aren't subtractors—we multiply the dream. But rejection… that's my fear, never belonging."

Jamal felt a pang. In Minneapolis, he'd seen families torn apart by ICE raids, dreams deferred by walls both physical and invisible. "Then let's erase those lines. Your contributions balance the equation. What if we build bridges instead?"

Carlos laughed, a witty spark returning. "Bridges? Now you're talking my language. Inclusion means no one left on the other side."

Another crack spiderwebbed across the cage.

Alex's turn. Their form shifted restlessly, colors clashing in protest. "Jamal, I'm the spectrum—the rainbow that defies black and white. My fear is forced conformity, losing my truth in a judgmental world. But I motivate for liberty's blessings to cover all expressions."

Jamal recalled whispers in school hallways, friends hiding their true selves. "Then shine, Alex. Your vulnerability empowers us. How does your fluidity recalibrate the variables?"

Alex's empathy flowed like a river. "By showing that equality isn't sameness—it's honoring differences. Without Inclusion, we're all dimmed."

The cage groaned, more fissures appearing.

Elara, tenacious and compassionate, stepped forward next. "I've labored in shadows, overlooked because of my gender, race, class. My efforts exploited, no reward. But I defy it—demand equity in opportunities."

"Theo," Jamal continued, turning to the Shackled. His reflective humor masked brooding pain. "Chains of incarceration… you represent the cycles that trap Black lives like mine. But redemption is possible. Break them with restorative justice."

Nia the Echo's voice amplified last, insightful and adaptive. "I'm the unheard, dismissed as burden. Ensure accessibility, make 'We' universal."

As each spoke, the cage weakened, but it wasn't enough. The Divider hovered, his manipulative charm twisting. "Touching speeches, but words aren't algebra. You need a catalyst."

That's when Ms. Harmony intervened, her resolute humor cutting through. "The catalyst is solidarity, Divider. Intersectional—where arcs cross, strength multiplies."

Jamal's mind sparked. Brainstorming equity: affirmative action as balancing factors, education reform as recalibrating variables. "Everyone, link hands! Form a coalition. We're not separate terms—we're an equation together."

They reached through the cracks, fingers intertwining allegorically. Lila's roots grounded them, Carlos's bridges connected, Alex's spectrum colored the links vibrantly. Elara's strategy wove the pattern, Theo's redemption strengthened the bonds, Nia's amplification echoed their unity.

A surge of energy pulsed. The Preamble Guardians appeared faintly—Jefferson's conflicted regret, Washington's stoic doubt, Madison's analytical hindsight—watching from the shadows, their arcs hinting at future allyship.

But intrigue deepened. As the cage shattered, a hidden mechanism revealed: illusions within illusions. The Divider had embedded spies—whispers of doubt that slithered into their minds.

"See?" a voice hissed in Jamal's ear. "Alex changes too much—unreliable."

Alex faltered, their colors dulling. "Is it true? My fluidity… a weakness?"

"No!" Jamal shouted, fiery determination igniting. "That's the Divider's twist. Your change is strength—adapting, evolving. In America, LGBTQ+ fights have sparked revolutions. Stonewall wasn't conformity; it was defiance!"

Alex's empathy surged back, vulnerability turning to power. "Then let's spectrum the algebra. Rewrite binaries into infinities."

Together, they brainstormed: Affirmative action = adding weights to tipped scales. Education reform = teaching history unwhitewashed, including all voices. Policy changes = criminal justice as restorative, not punitive.

The ground shifted, Equatoria's plains transforming into a grand algebraic arena. Equations floated like holograms: We the People + Diversity = Innovation. Minus Humanity = Dehumanization. Inclusion x Justice = Perfect Union.

But The Divider struck back, summoning storms of inequality—greater-than gusts that separated them. "You think coalitions last? History says otherwise—divides conquer!"

Intrigue peaked: A betrayal? Theo's fears resurfaced, his chains rattling. "What if I relapse? Society rejects the shackled."

Elara's compassion shone. "No, Theo. Your past redefines value. We're all flawed variables—together, we balance."

Nia's voice echoed, amplifying: "Accessibility for one lifts all."

Carlos quipped, "Even borders can't stop this familia."

Lila's poetry wove: "From erased lands, we reclaim."

Ms. Harmony nodded. "Intergenerational—my marches to your future."

Jamal, leader emerging, declared: "Harmony demands solidarity. Black, Brown, White, all united. Embracing Inclusion weaves diverse threads."

Alex, focus of the chapter, stepped center. Their form expanded, a prism splitting light into rainbows that pierced the storm. "I'm the proof. Without my spectrum, the equation is binary—zero or one, win or lose. But with me, it's infinite possibilities."

The Divider recoiled, his fear exposed: unity dismantling his power.

As the storm cleared, the group stood unbroken. They had rallied, formed coalitions. But whispers lingered—deeper challenges ahead.

Jamal glanced at Alex, gratitude swelling. "You empowered us through vulnerability. Self-acceptance in harmony."

Alex smiled, colors stable yet fluid. "And you showed me my place in the equation."

Ms. Harmony placed a hand on Jamal's shoulder. "This is just the algebra's beginning. Next, we rewrite the rules."

The chapter closed on a cliffhanger: A distant rumble—Preamble Guardians stirring, The Divider plotting. Intrigue built: What compromises would Madison reveal? How would Washington's reluctance test them?

Yet hope flickered. In this forging of balance, "We the Equal" felt closer. Diversity strengthened, Humanity bonded, Inclusion practiced, Justice founded. Without them, no perfect Union. With them? A nation reborn.

CHAPTER 8: REWRITING THE RULES

In the swirling mists of Equatoria, where numbers danced like fireflies and equations stretched across the horizon like ancient bridges, Jamal Thompson stood at the precipice of rebellion. The air hummed with the electric tension of unfinished calculations, the kind that left variables dangling, unresolved, begging for balance. He was no longer the wide-eyed boy from Northside Minneapolis, doodling equal signs in his notebook while sirens wailed outside his window. Now, at twelve years old, he was a force—a young mathematician of the soul, armed with the unyielding logic of fairness and the fire of those who had been deemed "less than" for far too long.

The group—Jamal's unlikely alliance of the Unequals—huddled in the shadow of the Great Ledger, a towering monolith etched with America's fractured history. Lila the Forgotten, her eyes like deep wells of ancestral memory, traced invisible patterns on the ground, whispering of stolen lands. Carlos the Bordered paced restlessly, his fingers twitching as if dismantling invisible walls. Alex the Spectrum shifted forms subtly, a kaleidoscope of colors reflecting the fluid beauty of identities long suppressed. Theo the Shackled rubbed his wrists, the phantom chains of incarceration still echoing in his brooding gaze. Nia the Echo sat quietly, her voice a resonant hum that amplified the group's whispers into thunder. And Ms. Harmony, ever the anchor, stood beside Jamal, her lined face a map of marches and midnight vigils, her gentle humor a shield against despair.

But it was Elara the Overlooked who commanded the moment. She had emerged from the underbelly of Equatoria like a shadow given form—tall and unyielding, her skin the rich hue of earth after rain, her eyes sharp as the edge of a forgotten blade. Women like her, women of color trapped in the grinding gears of poverty, were the invisible architects of society, their labors the unseen mortar holding up empires built on their backs. Elara's personality was a storm wrapped in silk: tenacious, compassionate, with a quiet defiance that could shatter glass. She had spent chapters lurking in the peripheries, challenging imbalances with subtle jabs—a word here, a strategy there. Now, in this chapter of forging balance, she would rise as the strategist, her arc bending toward empowerment, lifting voices that had been silenced for generations.

The Divider loomed before them, his form a swirling vortex of distorted symbols—greater-than signs twisted into whips, less-than arrows piercing the air like daggers. His charismatic chill seeped into the atmosphere, a sly intellect that had rigged every equation in Equatoria to favor the privileged. "You dare rewrite the rules?" he sneered, his voice a silken thread laced with venom. "The math of this land is eternal. Meritocracy is the great equalizer—those who work hard rise, those who don't… well, they were never meant to."

Jamal's heart pounded, but he stepped forward, his small frame casting a long shadow in the ethereal light. "Meritocracy?" he echoed, his voice steady despite the fear gnawing at his innocence. "That's just another myth you peddle, like saying everyone starts at the same line when some are born miles behind, shackled by history."

Elara placed a hand on his shoulder, her touch warm and grounding. "Let me show you, child," she murmured. Her motivations burned bright: to highlight the unseen labors, to demand equity in opportunities that had been denied to women like her—mothers scrubbing floors at dawn, sisters stitching dreams from scraps, aunts weaving communities

from threads of resilience. Her fear of perpetual invisibility
fueled her, but today, it would transform into strategy.
As the group formed a circle around the Great Ledger, the
allegory unfolded like a grand equation begging for revision.
The Ledger's surface shimmered, revealing the Preamble
etched in glowing script: We the People of the United States,
in Order to form a more perfect Union… But beneath it,
hidden variables pulsed—inequities coded into the core,
warping the promise into a lie.
"Look here," Elara said, her voice cutting through the haze.
She traced a finger across the stone, and symbols leaped to
life: a plus sign bloated with privilege, a minus devouring
resources from the margins. "This is the illusion of equality.
Policies that claim fairness but bake in bias—education
funded by property taxes, so rich neighborhoods get marble
halls while ours crumble. Justice systems that punish poverty
as if it's a crime, locking away fathers and sons while the
wealthy walk free."
Theo nodded, his reformed humor flickering. "I've felt those
chains. Mass incarceration isn't justice; it's a business built
on Black and Brown bodies."
The Divider laughed, a sound like cracking ice. "Justice? It's
served equally to those who deserve it. Your 'oppressions'
are excuses."
But Jamal, drawing on his love for math, saw the flaw. "No,"
he countered, his analytical mind whirring. "In a true
equation, you account for all variables. Meritocracy ignores
the starting lines—redlining that stole wealth from families
like mine, borders that trap dreamers like Carlos, norms that
erase Alex's truth. Without equity, it's not merit; it's rigged."
Intrigue thickened as whispers echoed from the
Ledger—ghostly voices of history, murmuring of Jim Crow, of
internment camps, of stolen children. The ground trembled,
and visions flashed: Elara as a young woman in the real
world, juggling three jobs in a city that overlooked her
brilliance, her ideas dismissed in boardrooms dominated by

faces unlike hers. "I've been the shadow," she confessed to the group, her compassion shining through. "Cooking, cleaning, caring—unseen work that props up the 'successful.' But no more."

Ms. Harmony smiled faintly. "Remember the March on Washington? We fought for jobs and freedom, but the fight's not done. Equity means lifting those overlooked, not just opening doors but building ramps where walls stand."

The confrontation escalated. The Divider summoned illusions—mirages of "self-made" heroes, bootstraps dangling temptingly. "Pull yourselves up!" he taunted. But Lila stepped in, her poetic insight weaving through the deception. "You stole the land for those boots. Without restorative justice, your equation is theft disguised as triumph."

Carlos grinned wryly. "And my people? We cross deserts for a dream, only to be bordered out. Contributions ignored, families torn."

Alex shimmered, their form stabilizing into a radiant prism. "Liberty for some means conformity for others. My spectrum isn't a threat—it's the color that makes the Union vibrant."

Nia's echo amplified: "And me? Dismissed as a burden. But accessibility isn't charity; it's inclusion, making 'We' truly universal."

Jefferson, the Flawed Founder, hovered nearby, his eloquent regret palpable. "I wrote of equality while holding men in bondage. Amend it—rewrite with truth."

Washington and Madison nodded, their stoic and strategic presences lending weight. "The compromises fractured us," Madison admitted. "Revise for inclusivity."

Elara took center stage, her quiet defiance blooming into command. "Let's rewrite," she declared. With a wave, the Ledger cleared, and a massive equation materialized: We the People = Perfect Union.

"But it's incomplete," Jamal said, his optimism flaring. "Add the variables."

Together, they inscribed: We the People + Diversity (varied perspectives fueling innovation) + Humanity (empathy binding us) + Inclusion (deliberate invitation for all) + Justice (fairness redressing wrongs) + Equity (balancing starting lines).

The Divider recoiled. "This disrupts the order!"

"Order built on lies," Elara shot back. Her arc peaked here—from laboring shadow to reform strategist. She debunked the meritocracy myth with precision: "Imagine a race where some start with weights, others with wings. Equity gives fair starts—affirmative action as balancing factors, criminal justice reform as unshackling potentials."

Real-world ties surged through the allegory: visions of policy battles—bills for reparations, equal pay acts for women of color, reforms dismantling the school-to-prison pipeline. Jamal saw his Minneapolis community center revived, funded equitably, teaching kids like him that their value wasn't conditional.

Intrigue deepened as The Divider struck back, summoning a labyrinth of twisted logic—false equivalences, gaslighting whispers. "Diversity divides!" he hissed.

"No," Jamal countered, using math logic. "Diversity multiplies strength. Like in algebra, varied terms create robust solutions."

The group navigated the maze, each character's fear confronted: Elara's invisibility shattered by her voice leading the way; Theo's relapse averted by collective support; Nia's isolation bridged by amplified echoes.

As they emerged, the equation transformed: We the People + Equity = We the Equal.

The Ledger glowed, cracks healing. Justice infused as the equalizer—accountability for the powerful, opportunities for the overlooked.

But depth came in the quiet moments. Jamal turned to Elara. "Why do you fight so hard?"

Her eyes softened. "Because I've been the one mopping up after the 'equals.' Poverty intersects with my race, my gender—triple binds. But in rewriting, I see my daughter free."

Humanity shone: shared vulnerabilities, empathy forging bonds.

Inclusion wove them: every voice shaping the new rules.

Diversity enriched: a mosaic stronger than monochrome.

The chapter built to a crescendo. The Divider, exposed in his fragility, shrank. "Unity will be your undoing!"

"No," Ms. Harmony said. "It's our salvation."

As the equation solidified, Equatoria shifted—bridges forming, scales balancing. Jamal felt the pull back to reality, but empowered, knowing this was no dream. It was a blueprint.

Yet intrigue lingered: whispers of backlash in the trials ahead. The revolution wasn't won; it was ignited.

CHAPTER 9: THE POWER OF EMPATHY

In the swirling mists of Equatoria, where equations danced like fireflies in the twilight and variables whispered secrets to the wind, Jamal Thompson felt the weight of his journey pressing upon him like an unbalanced scale. The realm had shifted since their grand rewrite in the previous chamber—a vast hall of mirrors where reflections twisted truths into lies, now left behind as a crumbling ruin. The Divider's influence lingered, though, in the air thick with doubt, and the group pressed onward through a labyrinth of fractured paths, each fork symbolizing the choices that had divided America for centuries.

Jamal, at twelve years old, had grown in ways he couldn't quantify. His once-childlike wonder for the equal sign had evolved into a fierce determination, a flame kindled by the stories of those around him. Lila the Forgotten walked beside him, her steps light on the earth that seemed to remember her ancestors' footprints. Carlos the Bordered cracked jokes to lighten the mood, his wit a shield against the invisible walls that still haunted his dreams. Alex the Spectrum shimmered with every hue of the rainbow, adapting to the group's energy like a chameleon in a storm. Elara the Overlooked marched with purpose, her eyes scanning for overlooked details in the maze. Nia the Echo followed, her voice resonating ahead to scout dangers, amplifying the faintest whispers into warnings. And then there was Theo the Shackled, trailing slightly behind, his chains—now metaphorical but no less real—clinking softly in his mind. Ms. Harmony, ever the guiding light, led the way with the Preamble Guardians in tow. Jefferson the Flawed Founder debated philosophy under his breath, his eloquent words laced with regret. Washington the Reluctant scanned the horizons like a general surveying a battlefield, his stoic facade cracking with unspoken doubts. Madison the Architect sketched invisible blueprints in the air, strategizing their next move with analytical precision.

But it was Theo who drew Jamal's attention that day. The man—allegorical embodiment of the formerly incarcerated, his form a mosaic of shadows and light—seemed more brooding than usual. His humor, usually a redeeming spark, had dimmed. As they navigated a particularly treacherous section of the labyrinth, where paths narrowed into tight squeezes that forced them to confront their own reflections, Theo lagged further. Jamal slowed his pace, falling back to walk beside him.

"You okay, Theo?" Jamal asked, his voice echoing off the mirrored walls. In Equatoria, sounds had a way of multiplying, like variables in an unsolved equation.

Theo glanced down, his eyes—a deep, reflective brown that held the weight of unseen prisons—meeting Jamal's with a flicker of surprise. "Okay? Kid, in this place, 'okay' is just another illusion. Like those mirrors showing us what we want to see instead of what's real."

Jamal nodded, thinking of his own reflections back home in Northside Minneapolis. The police stops, the underfunded schools, the way his mom's weary smile hid the exhaustion of working two jobs. "Yeah, but we're changing that, right? Rewriting the rules, like in the last chamber."

Theo chuckled, a low rumble that carried a hint of bitterness. "Rewriting's one thing. Living it? That's the real test. Chains don't break easy, Jamal. They rust, they wear, but they remember."

The group paused at a crossroads, where four paths diverged like the arms of a plus sign gone awry. Ms. Harmony consulted with the Guardians, their voices a murmur of historical echoes. "This labyrinth tests our bonds," she said, her gentle humor surfacing. "Remember the March on Washington? We didn't know the path, but we walked it together. Empathy was our compass."

As they deliberated, a sudden tremor shook the ground. The mirrors cracked, and from the fissures emerged spectral figures—ghosts of past injustices, allegorical wraiths that whispered accusations. "You don't belong," one hissed at Carlos, evoking border walls. "Forgotten and forsaken," another taunted Lila, stirring memories of stolen lands. The air grew cold, and the group huddled closer.

Theo froze, his face paling as a particular wraith approached him—a shadowy doppelganger clad in prison stripes, rattling chains that sounded like judgment. "Relapse," it sneered. "You'll always be shackled. Society rejects you. Why fight for a union that locked you away?"

Jamal watched as Theo's brooding intensity deepened, his fists clenching. This was the fear Theo carried: the relapse into old systems, the eternal rejection. But in that moment, something stirred in Jamal—a pull toward understanding, beyond his own pain. He stepped forward, placing a small hand on Theo's arm. "Hey, that's not you anymore. Tell me your story, Theo. Like Ms. Harmony says, sharing heals."

The group formed a circle, the wraiths circling like vultures but held at bay by their unity. Ms. Harmony nodded encouragingly. "Empathy, child. It's the bridge in the equation where humanity meets justice. Without it, diversity is just noise, inclusion a empty seat at the table."

Theo hesitated, his reformed humor flickering back like a candle in the wind. "Alright, kid. But stories like mine ain't pretty. They're the kind with no equal sign at the end—just imbalances stacked high."

He began, his voice steady but laced with emotion. Theo spoke of his allegorical origins: born into a system rigged from the start, a young Black man in America where the math of opportunity favored the privileged. "I was a variable they deemed less than," he said. "One mistake—a desperate choice in a world of few options—and the chains came down. Mass incarceration, they call it. But it's a divider's tool, locking away potential, breaking families, perpetuating the myth that some are inherently unequal."

As Theo wove his tale, the labyrinth responded. Visions projected on the mirrors: crowded prisons like overcrowded equations, where Black and Brown bodies outnumbered others disproportionately. "Thirteen percent of the population," Theo continued, "but nearly forty percent behind bars. That's not justice; that's a warped scale. And when I got out? The chains followed. No vote, no job, no second chance. Society's rejection is the real prison."

Jamal listened, his analytical mind piecing it together. He saw parallels to his own life—the fear in his neighborhood when sirens wailed, the way friends like him were profiled as threats before proven innocent. "But you're here now," Jamal said. "Fighting with us. That means something."

Theo's eyes softened. "Yeah, but fear's a sneaky thing. Relapse whispers when you're alone. What if I slip? What if the world never sees me as equal?"

The wraiths grew bolder, their whispers turning to shouts. One lunged at Theo, but Alex the Spectrum intervened, their form shifting to absorb the blow. "We all have spectra of pain," Alex said, vibrant colors pulsing. "Mine's the binary world that erases who I am. But empathy lets us see the full rainbow."

Lila chimed in, her poetic insight flowing like a river. "My people's stories were erased, lands stolen. Without humanity, we're just footnotes in someone else's equation."

Carlos nodded, his wit sharpening. "Borders kept me out, but empathy builds bridges. Deportation's shadow? It's real, but together, we shorten it."

Elara, tenacious as ever, added, "Women like me, overlooked in poverty's grip—our labors unseen, our voices silenced. Inclusion demands we listen, truly."

Nia the Echo amplified their words, her resonant voice making them boom. "Dismissed as burdens, we disabled are echoes unheard. But empathy turns volume up."

The Preamble Guardians observed, Jefferson's regret deepening. "I wrote of liberty while holding slaves," he admitted. "Hypocrisy blinded me to humanity."

Washington, reluctant no more, spoke up. "I led, but ignored divisions. Land theft scarred the union from the start."

Madison, analytical, sketched a new blueprint. "Compromises fractured us. Justice requires rewriting with empathy at the core."

Ms. Harmony, with her battle-hardened resolve, tied it together. "Remember the March? I was there, young and full of fire. Dr. King spoke of dreams, but it was empathy that marched us forward—seeing each other's humanity beyond color, class, creed."

As the circle tightened, Jamal felt a surge. This was the power of empathy: not just feeling, but acting on shared humanity. He turned to Theo. "Your story's part of mine now. We're not shackled alone."

Theo's brooding lifted, replaced by a genuine smile. "Kid, you got the fire. Restorative justice—that's my motivation. Redefining value beyond mistakes. Maybe, with empathy, we break the cycle."

The wraiths faltered, their forms flickering. But intrigue deepened as a hidden door revealed itself in the mirrors—a portal to a chamber of echoes, where past traumas replayed like looped equations. The Divider's voice echoed from within: "Empathy? A weakness! Division is strength!"

The group entered, the air thick with intrigue. Inside, holographic scenes unfolded: Theo's incarceration replayed, but intertwined with others' pains. Jamal saw his own potential future—a boy like him, profiled, imprisoned for minor offenses. "This is what happens without justice," Theo said, his voice steady. "But watch."

They interacted with the holograms, empathizing to alter them. Jamal approached a young holographic Theo, offering words of understanding. "You're more than your mistake." The scene shifted—the chains loosened.

One by one, they confronted intertwined traumas. Lila reclaimed land in a vision of restorative talks. Carlos dismantled a border wall with shared stories. Alex expanded binary boxes into spectra. Elara illuminated overlooked labors, demanding recognition. Nia amplified silenced needs, turning burdens into assets.

The Guardians joined, amending their legacies. Jefferson freed enslaved figures in the hologram, whispering apologies. Washington relinquished control, supporting indigenous returns. Madison revised compromises, infusing equity.

Ms. Harmony shared her March story vividly: the heat of August 1963, the sea of faces—Black, White, diverse—in unity. "We sang, we marched, we empathized. That's when change sparked."

Depth built as Theo faced his deepest fear: a hologram of relapse, society rejecting him post-release. "No job, no home, back to the streets," the wraith taunted.

But the group rallied. "We see you," Jamal declared. "Your value equals ours."

Tears glistened in Theo's eyes—vulnerability cracking his brooding shell. "Redemption-seeking humor aside, this… this heals."

The chamber trembled, the holograms dissolving into light. A new equal sign etched itself on the wall, balanced by empathy's bridge. The Divider's influence weakened further, his cold charisma no match for shared humanity.

As they exited, Theo walked taller, his arc bending toward advocacy. "From shackled to spokesperson," he quipped. "Thanks to you all."

Jamal felt transformed, empathy now his tool. "True union heals through listening," he echoed Ms. Harmony's words.

But intrigue lingered—a distant rumble hinted at trials ahead. The labyrinth wasn't done; backlash awaited in the next chamber. Yet, with empathy's power, they pressed on, forging toward "We the Equal."

CHAPTER 10: TRIALS OF TRANSFORMATION

In the swirling mists of Equatoria, where equations danced like fireflies and inequalities loomed like jagged cliffs, Jamal Thompson felt the weight of the world pressing down on his young shoulders. The realm, once a playground of mathematical wonders, had transformed into a labyrinth of trials, each twist and turn testing the fragile alliance he had forged. The air hummed with the echoes of their recent victories—the coalitions built in hidden algebraic groves, the rules rewritten on scrolls of shimmering code, the empathy that had begun to mend the fractures in their collective soul. But victory, Jamal was learning, was not a straight line; it was a equation fraught with variables, and now, those variables were rebelling.

The group—Jamal's ragtag band of Unequals, guided by Ms. Harmony and the reformed Preamble Guardians—had gathered in the heart of the Puzzle Plains. This vast expanse stretched before them like an unfinished mosaic, tiles of iridescent stone scattered across the ground, each one etched with symbols representing lives, histories, and identities. The plains were bordered by towering walls of warped equal signs, bent into mocking inequalities by The Divider's lingering influence. Overhead, storm clouds gathered, crackling with the energy of backlash, as if the very fabric of Equatoria resisted their progress.

Jamal wiped sweat from his brow, his twelve-year-old frame aching from the journey. "We can't stop now," he said, his voice steady but laced with the fire of determination. His eyes, once wide with childlike wonder at the equal sign's magic, now burned with the analytical intensity of a boy who had seen too much. Around him stood his companions: Lila the Forgotten, her resilient form cloaked in the earthy hues of forgotten lands; Carlos the Bordered, his resourceful grin masking the scars of invisible walls; Alex the Spectrum, shifting colors like a living rainbow, embodying the fluid beauty of authenticity; Elara the Overlooked, her tenacious gaze piercing through the shadows of neglect; Theo the Shackled, his reformed shoulders broad from carrying the weight of past chains; and Nia the Echo, whose insightful presence resonated like a distant bell, amplifying whispers into roars despite her own unseen struggles.

Ms. Harmony leaned on her staff, carved from the wood of ancient protest signs, her wise eyes scanning the horizon. "Child, the path to a perfect union ain't paved with ease. Remember the Preamble—it's a call to form, to establish, to ensure. But without trials, there ain't no transformation."

The Preamble Guardians hovered nearby, ethereal yet grounded in their remorse. Jefferson the Flawed Founder paced with eloquent strides, his conflicted idealism warring with regret. "We penned words of liberty," he murmured, "yet built them on hypocrisy. Now, we amend."

Washington the Reluctant stood stoic, his commanding presence tempered by doubt. "Leadership means facing the divisions we ignored. I see that now."

Madison the Architect nodded analytically, his perfectionist mind already calculating the next move. "The framework must be revised, inclusively."

But it was Nia who drew Jamal's attention most in this moment. She sat slightly apart, her form translucent, like a voice made visible—resonant yet often overlooked. Her personality was a blend of insight and adaptation; she could echo the needs of others, amplifying their truths, but her own challenges made her fear dismissal. "I hear the puzzle calling," she said softly, her words rippling outward like waves in a pond. "It's not just stones—it's us. Pieces that fit only when we value each other's shapes."

The Puzzle Plains were no ordinary field. As the group approached the central enigma—a colossal jigsaw where each piece pulsed with life—they felt the ground tremble. This was the allegory Ms. Harmony had warned of: a massive puzzle where people were the pieces, fitting only when valued equally. It represented America's grand equation, the "We the People" that demanded Diversity as its pattern, Humanity as its glue, Inclusion as its assembly, and Justice as its completion. Without these, the puzzle remained scattered, a fractured union mocking the Preamble's promise.

Suddenly, the storm broke. From the clouds descended shadowy figures—manifestations of backlash, born from those who feared change. They were the Whispers of Resistance, spectral beings shaped like twisted variables, their voices hissing doubts and divisions. "Why alter the equation?" one sneered, circling Carlos. "Borders keep the pure intact."

Another targeted Alex, its form rigid and binary. "Spectrums dilute strength. Conform or fade."

Elara faced a swarm that mocked her labors. "Overlooked? Rightfully so—your place is in the shadows."

Theo's chains rattled anew as a Whisper coiled around him. "Once shackled, always broken. Redemption is a myth."

Lila felt the pull of erasure, a void threatening to swallow her stories. "Forgotten lands mean forgotten people. Stay buried."

And Nia—poor Nia—the Whispers swarmed her most fiercely, their echoes drowning her own. "Echo? You're just noise, a burden in the silence."

Jamal's heart raced. These were not mere enemies; they were the internalized fears of a nation, the backlash against progress. As the Whispers attacked, the puzzle pieces began to scatter further, repelled by the discord. Jamal dodged a tendril of doubt, his mind flashing to his real-world home in Northside Minneapolis—the underfunded schools, the police sirens, the community center on the brink. "This isn't just a dream," he shouted. "If we fail here, we fail everywhere!"

The group fought back, but the assault was relentless. Lila summoned vines from the earth, symbols of resilient legacies, ensnaring a Whisper. Carlos built makeshift bridges from fallen tiles, his wit turning barriers into paths. Alex shifted forms, confusing the rigid attackers with fluid grace. Elara organized a counter-strategy, her compassion fueling a web of support. Theo broke free with raw strength, his humor lightening the load: "I've been shackled before— this is just a bad rerun!"

Yet the Whispers adapted, feeding on doubts. Jamal felt it creeping in—his own fears surfacing. What if he, a mere boy obsessed with equal signs, wasn't enough? What if the "broken math" of America was unfixable? He stumbled, a Whisper wrapping around his mind: "Youth is weakness. Your innocence is gone; your fire will burn out."

Ms. Harmony stepped forward, her resolute humor shining. "Not on my watch, shadows. We've marched through worse." She chanted words from the March on Washington, her voice a beacon, but even she wavered as the storm intensified.

It was then that Nia rose, her adaptive spirit igniting. "No," she declared, her resonant voice cutting through the chaos. The Whispers paused, surprised by her amplification. Nia's motivations burned bright: to make "We the People" universal, accommodating all abilities. Her fear of isolation fueled her now— she would not be dismissed.

"Listen," she commanded, echoing the group's strengths. Her words bounced off the puzzle pieces, vibrating them into alignment. "Diversity isn't a flaw—it's the pattern that makes us whole." As she spoke, tiles representing varied cultures and identities began to click together, forming a vibrant mosaic.

The Whispers recoiled, but pressed on. Jamal, inspired, joined her. "Humanity binds us—dignity for all, beyond labels!" More pieces locked in, the glue of empathy holding firm.

"Inclusion invites every voice," Alex added, their empathetic fluidity weaving threads between tiles.

"Justice corrects the scales," Theo boomed, his reformed humor turning a key piece.

The puzzle started to take shape—a grand tableau of America reimagined, where Indigenous lands were honored, borders dissolved into welcomes, spectrums celebrated, labors recognized, chains shattered, echoes heard.

But the trials deepened. A massive chasm opened in the plains, swallowing pieces—the void of absent pillars. "How can a perfect union exist without Diversity, Humanity, Inclusion, and Justice?" Jamal echoed the essential question, his analytical mind racing.

The Whispers laughed. "It cannot. Surrender to the fracture." Jamal doubted again, visions blurring. Then, from the mist, ancestors appeared—not as ghosts, but as luminous equations, their forms etched in light. Martin Luther King Jr., his voice a thundering integral: "Injustice anywhere is a threat to justice everywhere." Harriet Tubman, a guiding vector: "I freed a thousand slaves; I could have freed a thousand more if only they knew they were slaves."

Their presence fueled Jamal, banishing the Whisper from his mind. "We won't surrender. We'll transform!"

Nia, at the center, amplified the visions. Her insightful voice echoed the ancestors' words across the plains, resonating with each Unequal. Lila reclaimed her tile, poetic insight filling the erasure. Carlos bridged the chasm, his determination proving belonging. Alex illuminated the spectrum, fierce protectiveness defying conformity. Elara strategized the fit, her defiance lifting the overlooked. Theo advocated for second chances, breaking residual chains.

The puzzle neared completion, but one piece remained elusive—Nia's own, a resonant crystal echoing needs. The Whispers focused on her: "Burden. Dismissed. Isolated." Nia's fear peaked, but she adapted. "No—I am the echo that unifies." She placed her piece, and the puzzle sealed with a brilliant flash. The chasm closed, the storm dissipated. The Whispers dissolved, their backlash quelled by collective value.

As the group stood amid the completed mosaic—a perfect union allegorized—Jamal turned to Nia. "You were the key. Your voice made us whole."

Nia smiled, her form solidifying. "We all were. Transformation comes when we bridge barriers into something greater."

Ms. Harmony nodded, her fears eased. "The Preamble lives through us now—Diversity strengthening, Humanity bonding, Inclusion practicing, Justice founding."

The Guardians bowed. Jefferson: "Redemption through action." Washington: "Unity mentored." Madison: "Framework revised."

Yet intrigue lingered. As the mosaic glowed, a hidden inscription revealed: "The revolution awaits, but The Divider's final stand approaches." Shadows stirred on the horizon, hinting at deeper conspiracies—perhaps remnants of old compromises, or new variables unseen.

Jamal felt the pull back to reality, his transformation deepening. In Northside Minneapolis, change beckoned. But first, the trials had forged them unbreakable.

The group pressed on, intrigue building. What secrets hid in Equatoria's core? Would their unity hold against the ultimate test?

CHAPTER 11: THE EQUAL REVOLUTION

The air in Equatoria hummed with the electric charge of impending storm, a symphony of unbalanced equations crackling like thunder across the vast, shifting landscape. Jamal Thompson stood at the precipice of the Great Divide—a colossal chasm that cleaved the realm in two, its edges jagged with twisted equal signs forged into iron spikes. Below, the void swirled with forgotten variables: numbers and symbols cast aside, their values deemed unworthy by The Divider's cruel calculus. Above, the sky was a canvas of fractured stars, each one a distant dream of unity, flickering as if pleading for redemption.

Jamal's heart pounded, a drumbeat echoing the rhythms of his ancestors—those who had marched, bled, and dreamed before him. At twelve years old, he felt the weight of centuries pressing upon his slight frame, yet it no longer crushed him. It fueled him. Beside him stood his allies, the Unequals and the Preamble Guardians, a tapestry of faces and forms that embodied America's unfinished promise. Lila the Forgotten, her eyes like ancient rivers carving through stone, clutched a staff woven from indigenous roots. Carlos the Bordered, his witty grin masking the scars of invisible walls, flexed his hands as if ready to dismantle barriers with bare fists. Alex the Spectrum shimmered in iridescent hues, a living rainbow defying binary shadows. Elara the Overlooked straightened her back, her compassionate gaze sharpening into a blade of defiance. Theo the Shackled rattled his broken chains like a talisman, his brooding intensity now a forge for redemption. Nia the Echo's voice resonated softly, amplifying the whispers of the overlooked into a chorus.

Ms. Harmony, ever the steadfast mentor, placed a weathered hand on Jamal's shoulder. "Child, this is the moment where equations rewrite themselves. Remember: harmony ain't given; it's seized."

And then there were the Guardians—ethereal figures flickering between history and myth. Jefferson the Flawed, his eloquent features etched with regret, nodded solemnly. Madison the Architect paced, his analytical mind sketching invisible blueprints for a new order. But it was Washington the Reluctant who commanded the center, his stoic presence like a mountain amid the chaos. Tall and broad-shouldered, cloaked in a spectral uniform frayed by time, he had evolved from the stern summoner of old judgments to a humbled guide. His eyes, once clouded by the heroic myths of his own making, now burned with doubt turned to resolve. "I led armies across frozen rivers," he rumbled, his voice like gravel under boots, "but never did I cross the divide of my own failings. Today, we bridge it together—or fall as one."

The Divider loomed on the far side of the chasm, a colossal shadow woven from smoke and deceit. His form shifted: one moment a charismatic orator in tailored suits, the next a cold mathematician with eyes like voided zeros. He had rigged Equatoria's core equation, siphoning value from the Unequals to inflate his own power. Twisted vines of inequality snaked from his fingertips, ensnaring the land, turning fertile fields into barren wastelands where only the "superior" variables thrived. "Fools!" his voice boomed, echoing across the divide like a warped theorem. "Equality is an illusion for the weak. 'We the People' was never meant for all—only the worthy. Surrender, and I'll grant you scraps from my balanced ledger."

Jamal's fists clenched. He thought of his Northside Minneapolis home: the community center shuttered by indifferent budgets, the police sirens that sang lullabies of fear, the math problems in school that promised fairness but delivered division. "No more scraps," he whispered, then shouted it: "No more!"

The rebellion ignited not with a battle cry, but with a question—a spark from Jamal's curious mind. "How can a perfect union exist without Diversity, Humanity, Inclusion, and Justice?" The words hung in the air, rippling through Equatoria like a seismic wave. The ground trembled, equations awakening from slumber. Symbols long suppressed—fractions of forgotten cultures, decimals of dismissed identities—began to stir, rising from the chasm's depths.

Washington stepped forward, his reluctant heart now ablaze. In the earlier trials of Equatoria, he had questioned his past: the land he claimed, stolen from Lila's people; the leadership that ignored the cries of the shackled like Theo. Chapters of doubt had carved him anew, from a mythic general to a mentor of unity. "I feared the nation's collapse," he confessed to the group, his voice cracking like old parchment. "Ignored divisions I helped sow. But no more reluctance. Let us charge—not as conquerors, but as equals."

With that, the revolution surged. Carlos, ever resourceful, hurled a makeshift bridge across the chasm—a lattice of interwoven threads symbolizing immigrant contributions, sturdy yet flexible. "Borders are lines on paper," he quipped, his optimism cutting through the tension. "We redraw them!" The group crossed, feet pounding in rhythm, a march that evoked the ghosts of Selma and Stonewall.

The Divider unleashed his first assault: waves of manipulated myths crashing like tsunamis. "Meritocracy!" he snarled, summoning illusions of level playing fields where starting lines were rigged. Elara the Overlooked charged through, her tenacious spirit shattering the facade. "Merit ignores the labor of the invisible!" she cried, her compassionate intellect exposing the myth's hollow core. Women like her, toiling in shadows of poverty and prejudice, had built the nation's backbone. As she struck, equations realigned, revealing hidden variables of gender and class equity.

Intrigue deepened as shadows stirred—whispers of betrayal. Theo the Shackled hesitated, his fears of relapse gripping him. The Divider's voice slithered into his mind: "Return to your chains, reformed fool. Society rejects your kind." Theo's brooding eyes met Jamal's, and in that gaze, humanity flickered. "No," Theo growled, his redemption-seeking humor emerging as a defiant laugh. "Second chances aren't given—they're taken!" He swung his chains like a whip, cracking the Divider's defenses, symbolizing restorative justice breaking cycles of incarceration.

Nia the Echo amplified the chaos, her insightful voice echoing through the realm. "Hear us!" she commanded, transforming barriers into bridges of accessibility. Her fear of dismissal as a burden dissolved in the collective roar; instead, she became the unifier, her adaptive resonance binding the group's diverse strengths.

The battle twisted with creative fury. Alex the Spectrum danced through the fray, their vibrant form shifting colors to blind the Divider's minions—binary enforcers who sought to erase fluidity. "Liberty for all expressions!" Alex declared, their empathetic fluidity empowering allies. Lila invoked ancestral spirits, her poetic insight summoning winds that whispered forgotten histories, eroding the Divider's foundation of erasure.

Ms. Harmony wove through it all, her nurturing resolve a beacon. "Remember the March," she urged, sharing visions of Washington in 1963, where dreams deferred ignited change. Her fear of forgotten sacrifices fueled her, bridging generations.

The Guardians joined the melee. Jefferson, eloquent regret in his eyes, debated the Divider mid-battle: "My words of liberty were stained by hypocrisy. But we amend them now!" Madison, perfectionist drive ablaze, sketched tactical equations, revising the framework for inclusivity.

But the true intrigue unfolded with Washington. As the group closed in, the Divider revealed a hidden snare: a mirror of illusions, forcing each to confront their deepest fears. For Washington, it was a vision of national collapse—rivers of blood from ignored inequities, land thefts unraveling the Union. "You failed then," the Divider taunted. "You'll fail now." Washington faltered, his commanding stoic cracking. Doubt surged: the heroic myth he clung to, built on stolen ground. But Jamal approached, his fiery determination a light.

"General," Jamal said, "leadership isn't about perfection. It's about relinquishing control for equity. Help us perfect the Union you started."

In that moment, Washington's arc culminated. From reluctant spectator to humble supporter, he shattered the mirror with a resounding blow. "No more ignoring divisions!" he bellowed. "We decentralize power—for all!"

The rebellion crested. Jamal, at the heart, rallied them: "Diversity is our mosaic, Humanity our bond, Inclusion our invitation, Justice our scale! Without them, the Preamble is empty—union impossible!"

The group converged, each arc intersecting: Lila's resilience reclaiming history, Carlos's hope dismantling borders, Alex's vibrancy embracing spectra, Elara's tenacity lifting voices, Theo's reflection granting redemption, Nia's insight amplifying all. Guardians amended legacies, Ms. Harmony bridged eras.

In a blaze of light, they overthrew the Divider. His form dissolved into smoke, his power redistributed—equations balancing at last.

Jamal stood victorious, declaring: "We the Equal, in order to form a more perfect Union!"

The realm transformed: chasms filled, symbols united. Parallels to Black Lives Matter flickered—protests, votes, education as tools for change.

Yet intrigue lingered: a whisper of the Divider's essence escaping, hinting at ongoing vigilance. Depth in victory's cost: scars healed but remembered.

As Equatoria stabilized, Jamal felt the pull back to reality, empowered to lead.

CHAPTER 12: A NEW EQUATION

The first light of dawn filtered through the cracked blinds of Jamal's bedroom window, casting elongated shadows across the faded posters of mathematicians and civil rights icons that adorned his walls. He stirred under the thin blanket, his heart pounding as if he'd just sprinted a mile. The dream—no, the journey—still clung to him like mist from a riverbank. Equatoria. The land where equations breathed, where symbols waged wars, and where the very fabric of America's promise had been unraveled and rewoven before his eyes.

Jamal sat up abruptly, his breath coming in shallow bursts. The room spun for a moment, the familiar clutter of math notebooks and crumpled homework assignments grounding him back to Northside Minneapolis. But something was different. He felt it in his bones, a shift as profound as solving an impossible proof. The equal sign, once a simple doodle in his margins, now pulsed with meaning—a bridge, a battle cry, a blueprint for revolution.

He glanced at the clock: 6:17 AM. School wouldn't start for hours, but sleep was impossible. Flashes assaulted him: The Divider's sneering face dissolving into smoke, the Unequals standing tall in their reclaimed light, and Madison the Architect, that spectral figure with his quill and blueprints, nodding in solemn approval as the final equation balanced. "We the Equal," Madison had whispered in those last moments, his voice echoing like thunder across Equatoria's vast plains. "This is the true perfection we've sought."

Jamal swung his legs over the bed, his bare feet hitting the cold floor. He needed to move, to act. The weight of the Preamble pressed on him—not as words on yellowed paper, but as a living mandate. "We the People… in Order to form a more perfect Union…" But how perfect could it be without the pillars they'd fought for? Diversity, the mosaic of voices that turned monotony into symphony. Humanity, the thread of empathy weaving through every soul. Inclusion, the open door that turned strangers into kin. Justice, the scale that righted every wrong. Without them, the Union was a house of cards, trembling in the wind of history's unresolved storms.

He dressed quickly, grabbing his backpack and stuffing it with notebooks, markers, and a dog-eared copy of the Constitution his mother had given him last birthday. As he crept down the stairs, avoiding the creaky third step, he heard the soft hum of the kitchen radio. His mother, already up for her early shift at the hospital, was stirring coffee. She looked up, her eyes tired but sharp.

"Jamal? You're up early. Everything okay?"

He hesitated, then nodded. "Yeah, Mom. Just… had a weird dream. But it was good. Really good."

She smiled, though worry lines etched her forehead.

"Dreams can be teachers. What'd it say?"

He sat across from her, the words tumbling out in a rush. He spoke of Equatoria, framing it as a story at first, but the passion in his voice betrayed the truth of it. The Unequals, the Guardians, the Divider's fall. And Madison, the one who'd helped rewrite the rules. "It's like, the Constitution was a start, but it's incomplete. We gotta add the equals sign to make it real."

His mother listened, her spoon pausing mid-stir. "Sounds like you've been thinking deep, baby. Ms. Harmony been filling your head with those old stories again?"

Jamal grinned. "Something like that."

By the time he left for school, a plan was forming. The community center— the one slated for closure in Chapter 6's crisis—was his starting point. It couldn't close. Not now. It would become the hub for something new: a youth program where kids like him learned equity through math and history. Equations that balanced real lives, not just numbers.

The streets of Northside buzzed with morning life as Jamal walked. The corner store where Mr. Ramirez sold fresh tortillas, the mural of George Floyd that still brought tears to passersby, the playground where kids of every color laughed without knowing the divides waiting for them. This was his Equatoria, raw and real. And he was ready to rewrite its equation.

At school, math class felt electric. Mr. Jenkins droned on about algebra, but Jamal's mind raced ahead. During break, he cornered his friends—Tyrell, whose family had faced eviction like in his visions; Sofia, the new girl from Mexico whose accent drew stares; and Jamie, who preferred they/them and kept to the shadows. "We gotta do something," he said, pulling out his notebook. "About the center closing. But more than that. A club. Math for Justice or something."

They stared, then nodded. Intrigue sparked in their eyes. By lunch, the group had grown. Whispers of a petition, a rally. Jamal felt Madison's presence, that strategic mind urging him: "Revise the framework. Make it inclusive."

But the day held a twist. As Jamal headed to the community center after school, he spotted a familiar figure outside: Ms. Harmony, her silver hair catching the afternoon sun, arguing with a suited man holding a clipboard. The developer, no doubt, eyeing the building for condos.

"Ms. Harmony!" Jamal called, jogging up.

She turned, her face lighting up. "Jamal, child. Just the one I need."

The developer scowled. "This property's as good as sold. Funding's dried up."

"Not if we fight it," Jamal said, his voice steady. Ms. Harmony's eyes widened at his newfound fire.

Inside the center, the air smelled of old books and fresh paint from last summer's mural project. Ms. Harmony gathered the staff— a mix of volunteers from the neighborhood: Mrs. Littlefeather, whose Lakota heritage mirrored Lila's quiet strength; Mr. Gonzalez, a immigrant advocate like Carlos; and others who embodied the Unequals he'd met.

"We can't let this go," Jamal said, standing on a chair to address them. "This place is our Equatoria—our chance to balance the scales."

Ms. Harmony chuckled. "Equatoria? Sounds like one of my old tales."

"It's more than that," he insisted. And then he told them everything, weaving the allegory into a call to arms. The room fell silent, then erupted in nods and ideas.

As the meeting progressed, Jamal felt a pull toward the back room, where dusty archives held neighborhood history. There, amid yellowed newspapers, he imagined Madison appearing—not as a ghost, but as inspiration. In Equatoria's final battle, Madison had been the key. While Washington led the charge and Jefferson debated ideals, Madison had drafted the new preamble: "We the Equal, in order to form a more perfect Union, establish Justice through Diversity, insure domestic Tranquility via Humanity, provide for the common defense with Inclusion, promote the general Welfare by equity, and secure the Blessings of Liberty to ourselves and our Posterity…"

Now, in the real world, Jamal picked up a pen. "We start with a program," he said aloud to the empty room. "Kids teaching kids. Math problems that solve real inequities. History lessons that honor the forgotten."

But intrigue lurked. As evening fell, a knock echoed at the center's door. The developer again, but with a twist—he wasn't alone. Beside him stood a city councilman, eyes narrowed. "Heard you're stirring trouble, kid."

Jamal's heart raced. This was The Divider's echo, the system fighting back. "We're not trouble," he replied, channeling his fiery determination. "We're the solution."

The councilman laughed, but Ms. Harmony stepped in, her resolute voice cutting through. "This center stays. We've got petitions starting, and media on the way."
The men left, grumbling, but Jamal knew it wasn't over. That night, as he helped organize flyers, doubts crept in—his fear of failure surfacing. What if it all crumbled?
In his dreams, Equatoria returned. Not the war-torn land, but a reborn one. The Unequals gathered in a grand hall, equations glowing on walls like constellations. Madison stood at the center, his perfectionist drive now fulfilled. "The arc bends," he said to Jamal. "But only if you pull."
Jamal awoke renewed. The next days blurred into action. The youth program launched informally: sessions where kids used math to map redlining districts, calculating the "inequality coefficients" of school funding. Sofia shared stories of border crossings, tying into Carlos's arc. Jamie led discussions on identity, echoing Alex's spectrum.
Word spread. Local news picked up the story—a 12-year-old leading a charge against gentrification. Protests formed, diverse crowds chanting "We the Equal!" Ms. Harmony beamed, her fear of forgotten sacrifices easing as youth took the mantle.
Yet depth came in quieter moments. One evening, Jamal visited Mrs. Littlefeather's home, where she showed him artifacts from her ancestors. "We've been forgotten," she said, her introspective voice mirroring Lila's. "But you're remembering us."
Similarly, Theo's real-world counterpart—a reformed ex-con mentoring at the center—shared his story of shackles broken. "Redemption ain't easy," he said with brooding humor. "But it's possible."
As the program grew, Jamal faced personal intrigue. A bully from school, echoing The Divider's manipulation, tried to sabotage a rally with rumors. "You think you're equal? Prove it." Jamal didn't fight; he invited him in. "Join us. See the equation."

The boy hesitated, then stayed. Transformation.
In the climax of this real-world arc, the city hearing arrived.
The center packed with supporters—immigrants, activists,
youth. Jamal spoke last, his analytical mind shining. "How
can a perfect union exist without Diversity, Humanity,
Inclusion, and Justice? It can't. We've seen it in history's
imbalances. But we can rewrite it."
The council, moved, voted to fund the center. Cheers
erupted.
In the epilogue's vision, Jamal stood on a hill overlooking a
harmonious America—not perfect, but progressing. Cities
where Diversity bloomed in every street, Humanity softened
every policy, Inclusion opened every door, Justice righted
every scale. The Preamble lived, evolved into "We the
Equal." As activists, we must live it daily. Harmony, our
birthright.

Years passed like pages turning in an unfinished manuscript.
Jamal's story, born from that transformative journey, didn't
fade into memory—it spread. What began as scribbled notes
in a community center evolved into a book, We The Equal, a
beacon that illuminated hidden fractures and inspired
awakenings across the nation. From the streets of
Minneapolis to the quiet libraries of distant estates, its
allegory reached unlikely hearts, challenging legacies and
forging unexpected alliances. One such heart belonged to a
boy in Virginia, whose inherited shadows would soon bend
toward the light...

CHAPTER 13: LEGACY EQUATION

In the crisp autumn time of the year, as leaves turned fiery reds and golds in the rolling hills of Virginia, Ethan Whitaker sat in the shadowed library of his family's estate, a sprawling mansion built on land that had once been a plantation. At 13, Ethan was the epitome of inherited privilege—tall for his age, with tousled blonde hair and blue eyes that mirrored the portraits of his ancestors lining the walls. Those eyes, however, held a restlessness, a quiet storm beneath the surface. He was intelligent, with a mind that devoured history books and puzzles, but his world had been carefully curated: private schools, polo lessons, and family dinners where conversations skirted the uncomfortable truths of their lineage.

Ethan's personality was a blend of inherited stoicism and budding curiosity. He was reserved, often observing rather than participating, his words measured like the strategic moves in the chess games he played with his grandfather. But beneath that, a spark of empathy flickered, kindled by fleeting moments—like the time he'd seen a Black classmate teased for his accent, or when his history teacher glossed over slavery with a wave of her hand. His motivation had always been simple: to uphold the family name, the Whitaker legacy of "pioneers" who "built America." Yet, deep down, he feared the cracks in that narrative—the dread that uncovering the past would shatter his sense of self, leaving him adrift in a world where his privilege was a curse rather than a crown.

The book We The Equal had arrived unannounced, slipped into his backpack by a mysterious substitute teacher who'd vanished as quickly as she'd appeared. "Read this," the note said. "The equation isn't balanced yet." Ethan had dismissed it at first, but boredom one rainy afternoon led him to crack it open. Jamal Thompson's story gripped him like a vice—the young boy's fascination with the equal sign, the dream portal to Equatoria, the battles against The Divider. As Ethan turned the pages, the allegory seeped into his consciousness, mirroring his own unspoken questions. Why did his family's wealth feel like a heavy chain? Why did the Preamble's words, recited in school, ring hollow when he thought of the old slave quarters hidden behind the estate's manicured gardens?

That night, as thunder rumbled outside, Ethan dreamed. Or was it a dream? The line blurred, much like in Jamal's tale. He found himself in Equatoria, not as an observer, but as a participant—a pale figure in a land of living equations, where numbers danced and symbols clashed. The air shimmered with mathematical precision, but distortions rippled through it, like heat waves over asphalt. He stood on a vast plain, where equal signs stretched like bridges across chasms, but many were twisted, bent by invisible forces.

"Who are you?" a voice echoed, resonant and wise. Ethan turned to see Ms. Harmony, her silver hair glowing under an ethereal light, her nurturing gaze piercing through him. In the book, she was Jamal's mentor; here, she seemed to see straight into Ethan's soul.

"I'm… Ethan," he stammered, his voice small. "I don't belong here."

Ms. Harmony's gentle humor surfaced in a soft chuckle. "Child, no one belongs until they choose to. But your blood calls you here—the blood of those who built the walls."

Before he could respond, shadows coalesced into forms—the Unequals. Lila the Forgotten emerged first, her resilient introspection like a quiet wind, her eyes holding the pain of erased histories. "Your ancestors took our land," she said, not accusingly, but factually, her poetic insight weaving images of stolen territories into the air.

Ethan recoiled, his fear surging. His great-great-grandfather had been a Confederate officer, owner of hundreds of acres worked by enslaved people. The family lore painted him as a "gentleman farmer," but Ethan had glimpsed old ledgers in the attic, names listed like inventory. "I didn't do that," he protested, but the words tasted like ash.

Next came Carlos the Bordered, his witty optimism cutting through the tension. "Borders aren't just walls; they're in minds too. Your family's fortunes came from excluding folks like me." Carlos's determination flashed as he gestured to a crumbling barrier in the distance, symbolizing the artificial divides his people faced.

Alex the Spectrum shimmered into view, their vibrant empathy enveloping Ethan like a warm light. "Liberty for some means conformity for others. Your legacy forced binaries on us all." Alex's fluid adaptability shifted their form slightly, a reminder of marginalized identities, and Ethan felt a pang—his own family had donated to politicians who opposed LGBTQ+ rights, all under the guise of "traditional values."

Elara the Overlooked stepped forward, her tenacious compassion burning bright. "We toiled in shadows while your kin reaped the rewards. Poverty isn't fate; it's designed." Her sharp intellect dissected the intersections of gender, race, and class, and Ethan thought of the women in his family's history—silenced, overlooked, even as the men prospered.

Theo the Shackled loomed, his brooding intensity softened by humor. "Chains don't break easy. Your ancestors built the prisons that hold us still." Theo's redemption-seeking arc mirrored Ethan's budding guilt, the fear of relapse into ignorance.

Nia the Echo's voice resonated without form at first, amplifying the others. "Dismiss us as burdens, and the equation fails. Accessibility is humanity." Her insightful adaptation made Ethan confront his school's lack of ramps, the ableism woven into everyday life.

Then, the Preamble Guardians appeared—Jefferson, Washington, Madison—their forms spectral, their personalities conflicted. Jefferson's eloquent regret washed over Ethan. "I wrote of liberty while holding men in bonds. Amend my flaws, boy." Washington's stoic doubt cracked: "Leadership without equity leads to ruin." Madison's analytical hindsight urged: "Revise the framework; compromises fracture unions."

But the true intrigue unfolded when The Divider materialized, his manipulative charisma drawing Ethan in. "Why fight it?" The Divider whispered, his cold intellect twisting logic. "Your family earned this. Unity weakens the strong." Ethan felt the pull—the myth of superiority, the justification for imbalance. It was seductive, echoing his grandfather's dinner table rants about "meritocracy."

Yet, as the Unequals shared their stories, a collective consciousness stirred. Jamal appeared last, his fiery determination igniting the scene. "The equal sign doesn't discriminate. Join us, or stay divided."

In the dream's climax, Ethan faced a choice: a golden path of privilege or a bridged chasm leading to the Unequals. Intrigue deepened as he uncovered a hidden artifact—a rusted key from his family's past, symbolizing locked-away truths. Turning it unlocked visions: his ancestors' cruelties, the human cost, but also glimmers of redemption—distant relatives who'd aided abolitionists in secret.

Awakening in a sweat, Ethan knew the dream was more than fantasy. The book had awakened him, exposing the illusion of equality. His ancestors' ills—slavery, land theft, systemic oppression—were the roots of current disparities. But the pillars beckoned: Diversity as strength, Humanity as bond, Inclusion as practice, Justice as foundation.

The next day, Ethan confronted his family. His parents, descendants of wealth, dismissed his questions at breakfast. "History is history," his father said, a lawyer who'd defended corporations against discrimination suits. But Ethan's fear—of losing his family's approval—clashed with his motivation to atone.

Sneaking into the attic, he found the ledgers, letters revealing his great-grandfather's role in Jim Crow laws. Intrigue built as he discovered a hidden diary from a Whitaker aunt who'd smuggled escaped slaves north, her story erased to preserve the family myth. This duality fueled him—the legacy wasn't monolithic; redemption was possible.

At school, Ethan sought out diverse peers. He befriended a Black girl named Maya, whose family had roots in Minneapolis, echoing Jamal's world. "Read this," he said, lending her We The Equal. Their discussions deepened: How without Diversity, innovation stagnates; without Humanity, empathy dies; without Inclusion, voices silence; without Justice, resentment festers.

Ethan's arc accelerated when he learned of a local rally for reparative justice. His fear peaked— what if his family disowned him? But motivated by the book's hope through action, he attended, sign in hand: "We The Equal—Start with Justice."

There, intrigue twisted: he spotted his grandfather in the crowd, not protesting against, but quietly observing. Later, in a tense confrontation, the old man revealed his own awakening decades ago, suppressed by fear. "I failed to act. Don't repeat it."

Joining the collective, Ethan organized a youth group, implementing the pillars. They hosted diverse story circles (Diversity), empathy workshops (Humanity), inclusive policy drives (Inclusion), and justice campaigns for prison reform (Justice). White children like him, from similar backgrounds, joined, their consciousnesses stirred by the book.

In a pivotal moment, Ethan dreamed again, reuniting with the characters. "You've bridged the gap," Ms. Harmony said. The Divider faded, his power broken by unity.

As autumn deepened, Ethan's path led him northward, drawn by an invitation to a national event in Manhattan—the launch of We The Equal itself. There, he would meet Jamal, the boy from the book now a grown leader, their alliance a living testament to intersectionality and youth empowerment. The legacy equation had balanced, not by erasure, but by equity—and the story was far from over.

CHAPTER 14: ECHOES OF EQUATORIA

The autumn sun dipped low over Manhattan, casting a golden haze through the floor-to-ceiling windows of the bustling bookstore on Fifth Avenue. The air hummed with anticipation. Banners fluttered from the rafters, emblazoned with the bold title: We The Equal. Stacks of the book towered like monuments on display tables, their covers featuring a stylized equal sign morphing into a diverse crowd of hands clasped in unity. Jamal Thompson, now a lanky 22-year-old with a neatly trimmed beard and eyes that still sparkled with that childhood curiosity, sat at a long oak table, Sharpie in hand. He had grown into his frame, his once-boyish features sharpened by years of advocacy, but the fire—the one ignited in the dreamlike realm of Equatoria—still burned bright.

The line snaked through the store, a microcosm of America itself: young students clutching dog-eared copies, elderly activists with weathered signs from marches long past, immigrants with hopeful smiles, and skeptics with folded arms. Jamal signed each book with a personal flourish, often adding a quote from the Preamble or a quick sketch of an equal sign. "To Anaeya," he wrote in one, "Remember: Diversity isn't a checkbox; it's the equation's heartbeat." He handed it back with a warm grin, his voice carrying the rhythmic cadence of Northside Minneapolis, softened by years on the national stage.

But beneath the polished exterior of the New York Times bestselling author, Jamal felt a familiar tug—a whisper from the past. It had been ten years since that fateful night when a simple math problem had pulled him into Equatoria, the allegorical world where equations lived and breathed, where the Divider had twisted balance into bondage. The adventure had reshaped him, turning a wide-eyed 12-year-old into a force for change. He'd channeled it all into this book, a blend of memoir and manifesto, weaving his real-life awakenings with the fantastical tales of Lila the Forgotten, Carlos the Bordered, and the rest. We The Equal had debuted at number one, sparking debates in Congress, classrooms, and coffee shops. Yet, as the crowd swelled, Jamal couldn't shake the sense that the story wasn't finished. Equity wasn't a destination; it was a perpetual motion.

"Mr. Thompson, your work changed my life," said a young woman in line, her hijab framing a face alight with determination. She was perhaps 18, clutching a worn notebook. "I'm starting a diversity club at my school because of Chapter 5—the Weight of History. Lila's story… it's like she's speaking for my grandparents who fled Syria."

Jamal leaned forward, his analytical mind kicking in. "That's the point. History isn't a mountain we climb once; it's a path we pave together. What's your name?"

"Aisha," she replied, beaming as he inscribed her copy: "To Aisha, the next architect of inclusion. Keep echoing the unheard."

As she moved on, Jamal's thoughts drifted to Lila the Forgotten. In Equatoria, she'd been a shadowed figure, her resilient introspection a quiet storm against erasure. He'd met real Indigenous leaders since then, drawing from their wisdom to flesh out her arc. But tonight, intrigue lurked in the shadows of his success. Whispers had reached him through his agent: a conservative think tank was planning a counter-narrative, a book dismissing We The Equal as "divisive fiction." And then there was the anonymous email he'd received that morning: "The Divider never truly fades. Watch your back at the signing."

He shook it off, attributing it to trolls. Activism invited backlash; it was the price of progress. Yet, as the evening wore on, the crowd parted for a familiar face—Ms. Harmony, her silver hair now in elegant twists, leaning on a cane carved with equal signs. She was 78 now, but her nurturing resolve hadn't dimmed. "My boy," she said, enveloping him in a hug that smelled of lavender and old books. "Look at you, turning dreams into revolutions."

"Couldn't have done it without you, Ms. H," Jamal replied, his voice thick. In the book, she'd been his mentor, guiding him through Equatoria's trials. In reality, she'd been his community center director, the one who'd first handed him a copy of the Constitution. Her arc in the story mirrored her life: from civil rights marches to mentoring youth, finding renewed purpose in their victories.

They chatted briefly about the old neighborhood in Northside Minneapolis, where Jamal's youth programs now thrived—teaching equity through math workshops, just as he'd envisioned in the epilogue. But as Ms. Harmony stepped aside, a man approached, his suit crisp, his smile too polished. He was in his fifties, with a clipboard and a badge reading "Equity Watch Institute." Intrigue prickled Jamal's skin.

"Impressive turnout, Mr. Thompson," the man said, sliding a copy across the table. "I'm Dr. Elias Crowe. Your allegory is… creative. But does it address the real math? America's already equal under the law. Why stir division?"

Jamal's fiery determination surfaced, tempered by years of debates. "Equality under the law is the starting line, Dr. Crowe, but equity levels the track. Without it, the Preamble's 'perfect Union' is just words on parchment." He signed the book: "To Dr. Crowe, May the illusion shatter for us all."

Crowe leaned in, his voice low. "Careful. Some see your 'Divider' as a caricature. What if he's not the villain you paint? What if balance requires sacrifice from all sides?"

The words echoed like a ripple from Equatoria, where The Divider had manipulated with sly intellect, justifying imbalance with myths of merit. Jamal felt a chill. Was this man a mere critic, or something more? As Crowe melted into the crowd, Jamal spotted a young boy at the end of the line—about 12, African American, with a backpack slung low. He reminded Jamal of himself, all curiosity and unspoken questions.

The signing continued, each interaction layering depth to the night. A Latinx family approached, the father sharing how Carlos the Bordered had inspired him to advocate for immigration reform. "Your story broke down walls in my mind," he said. Jamal nodded, recalling Carlos's resourceful hope, his arc from entrapment to coalition-building. "Contributions from all origins strengthen us," Jamal replied, echoing the character's motivation.

Then came a non-binary teen, their eyes lighting up at the mention of Alex the Spectrum. "Chapter 7—Allies in the Algebra—made me feel seen," they said. "The way Alex empowers through vulnerability… it's me." Jamal's heart swelled; Alex's vibrant empathy had been drawn from real LGBTQ+ friends, their fear of invisibility transformed into self-acceptance.

As the line dwindled, intrigue deepened. A woman in a wheelchair rolled up—Nia the Echo incarnate, though she introduced herself as Lena. "Your portrayal of disability in Chapter 10 hit home," she said. "Unheard needs becoming bridges— that's what inclusion means." Jamal inscribed: "To Lena, amplify the echoes until all hear."

Ms. Harmony lingered nearby, her gentle humor cutting through the tension. "See? Your words are seeds, sprouting everywhere."

Yet, as the store lights dimmed, the young boy finally reached the table. His name was Malik, and his eyes held that same wonder Jamal once had for equal signs. "In your book, Equatoria feels real," Malik said shyly. "Did you really go there?"

Jamal paused, the boundary between allegory and memory blurring. "In a way, yes. It's the world inside all of us—the fight for balance." He signed Malik's copy with extra care: "To Malik, the next catalyst. Fix the broken math."

As Malik walked away, Jamal noticed Dr. Crowe lingering in the shadows, conversing with a shadowy figure. Paranoia? Or a sign that The Divider's fears—unity dismantling influence—were manifesting in reality?

As the crowd began to thin, a reserved young boy with tousled blonde hair approached the table, his blue eyes wide with a mix of curiosity and trepidation. Ethan Whitaker, clutched his well-worn copy of the book, its pages marked with notes from his attic discoveries and dream-inspired revelations. Jamal looked up, sensing something profound in the boy's stoic demeanor.

"You're Jamal, right? From the story," Ethan said, his voice measured but edged with budding empathy. "I'm Ethan. Your book... it showed me things about my family I didn't want to see. The walls we built, the chains we ignored. But it also showed me how to bridge them—with Diversity, Humanity, Inclusion, Justice."

Jamal's eyes lit up, recognizing the spark of transformation. "Ethan, that's the heart of it. The Power of Empathy! The equal sign doesn't care about where you start; it's about balancing the equation together. What part hit you hardest?"

"The Preamble Guardians," Ethan replied, his fear of shattering his legacy giving way to motivation. "Jefferson's regret—it's like my ancestors. I started a group back home, inviting everyone to share stories, to love across divides. But I'm scared... what if it's not enough?"

Jamal leaned in, sketching an equal sign on Ethan's copy. "It's enough if you act. Love isn't easy—it's the new command that changes everything. As I loved you and your relationship to the equations enough to add your realities to the book through empathy, love others. That's how we form a more perfect Union."

Ethan nodded, a quiet resolve settling in. "Thanks. I'll keep bridging."

As the line persisted, a determined man in his thirties approached, flanked by a group of teenagers aged 13 to 17, their expressions a mix of wariness and tentative hope. The man, Joshua, carried a stack of books, his posture radiating the quiet intensity of someone who'd spent years battling systemic tides. As a community activist dedicated to disrupting the school-to-prison pipeline, Joshua had seen too many young lives derailed by zero-tolerance policies, racial profiling, and underfunded schools funneling kids straight into the criminal justice system. Tonight, he'd brought these youths—each with their own run-ins with the law, from minor truancy charges to more serious brushes that could have sealed their fates—hoping Jamal's story might offer the guidance they desperately needed.

"Jamal Thompson," Joshua said, extending a hand with a firm grip, his voice steady and resonant. "I'm Joshua, from the National Youth Justice Network. I was in town, and decided to bring a few young people along with me to meet you; in hope that you might of some words of encouragement. Your book is a weapon against the pipeline—the way schools push kids like these into prisons instead of futures. Theo the Shackled? That's their story. I brought them here because they need to see someone who made it out."

Jamal's eyes softened as he looked at the group—four boys and two girls, shifting uncomfortably but listening intently. He recognized the haunted look in their eyes, the same one he'd carried as a kid, wondering if the "urban jungle" of Northside Minneapolis would swallow him whole. "Joshua, man, thank you for the work you're doing. Disrupting that pipeline—it's like rewriting the equation before it's too late. And you all," he said, turning to the teens with a voice thick with emotion, "I see you. I know what it feels like to wonder if you'll make it out unscathed, to feel like the system's rigged against you from the start. I was you—dodging traps, questioning if the math of life would ever add up. But listen: you are not your mistakes. You're the catalysts, the ones who can balance this. Grab hold of those pillars—Diversity in your stories, Humanity in your hearts, Inclusion in your circles, Justice in your fight. You've got the power to rewrite your arc, just like Theo did."

One of the boys, a 15-year-old with a faded scar on his cheek, met Jamal's gaze. "But how? They already got me on probation."

Jamal leaned forward, his fiery determination shining through. "Start small—build alliances, like in the book. Demand the equity you deserve. And remember, love one another through it. That's the command that breaks chains."

"You, young man have to determine to make better decisions despite the temptations to cross the chasms where the equal signs are broken and twisted. Those many times are the very place where you realize the error of your ways. He quoted an old Pastor of his, "Crooked roads waste time." and "When a mans way are pleasing to God, He will make even his enemies be at peace with him."

The group nodded, a spark igniting in their eyes as Jamal signed their books with personalized messages: "To Darius—Break the pipeline, build the bridge." He handed them back, clasping each hand firmly.

Turning back to Joshua, Jamal placed a hand on his shoulder. "You're doing the right thing, brother. Guiding them like this? It's the revolution we need. Keep disrupting— the equal sign is on your side."

Joshua smiled, a weight lifting. "Thanks, Jamal. We'll keep fighting."

After the signing, Jamal joined Ms. Harmony for coffee at a nearby café. The city pulsed outside, a symphony of diversity. "That Crowe fellow," she mused, "reminds me of the old guard. They fear what they can't control."

Jamal nodded, but his mind wandered to the Preamble Guardians: Jefferson's conflicted regret, Washington's stoic doubt, Madison's analytical hindsight. In the book, they'd evolved from flawed founders to allies in equity. "We can't amend legacies without action," Jamal said. "That's the hope through action."

Their conversation turned to the essential question: "How can a perfect union exist without Diversity, Humanity, Inclusion, and Justice?" Ms. Harmony smiled. "It can't, child. Without them, it's no union at all—just a fractured facade."

As they parted, Jamal stepped into the night, the weight of his books in his bag. But then, a flicker—a dreamlike shimmer in the alley. The numbers 11:11 glowed and dissipated as quickly as they appeared. Equatoria? He blinked, and it was gone. Or was it? Intrigue pulled him forward. Activism wasn't over; it was eternal.

Back in his hotel room, Jamal opened his laptop, drafting notes for a sequel. The story of We The Equal had inspired millions, but the real work lay ahead. He thought of Elara the Overlooked, her tenacious compassion demanding recognition for women of color in poverty. Of Washington relinquishing control, Madison revising frameworks. Their arcs intersected with his own, a testament to intersectionality.

A knock at the door startled him. It was Malik, breathless. "I forgot to ask—how do I start? How do I fight like you?" Jamal never lost his street smarts, so he looked out the door both ways before removing his foot from behind the door. Jamal asked, "How did you find my hotel room?" Malik felt in that moment that his decision to follow Jamal was a mistake. Malik spoke with a redemptive tone. "Sir, I want to be like you." Malik's eyes hung low like the branches of a willow tree. Feeling the uncertainty of his vulnerability, he stood motionless.

Jamal invited him in, the empowerment of youth reigniting. "Start with questions. Why doesn't the equation balance? Then act—build alliances, demand justice."

As they talked, Jamal realized this was the depth of his journey: not just writing the book, but living it. The intrigue of threats like Crowe only fueled him. For in the face of division, unity was the ultimate intrigue—the plot twist America needed. Alright Malik, that is all I have for you today. Jamal thanked Malik for coming to the book signing and told him to be safe as he made his way home. They both said, Peace! Malik bounced away as if every step sprung from an elastic equal sign.

The night deepened, and Jamal dreamed of Equatoria once more. The Unequals gathered, their voices a chorus: "We the Equal." He awoke renewed, ready to bridge more gaps.

In the months that followed, Jamal's activism evolved. He testified before Congress on equity reforms, drawing from the book's themes. Diversity as strength fueled his coalitions; Humanity bonded them; Inclusion invited all; Justice balanced the scales. When Crowe's counter-book launched, Jamal responded not with anger, but dialogue—hosting town halls where skeptics became allies.

One such event, in Minneapolis, reunited him with echoes of his past. A Indigenous elder, reminiscent of Lila, shared land reclamation stories. An immigrant activist, like Carlos, spoke of border humanity. The spectrum of voices—LGBTQ+, disabled, formerly incarcerated—wove a tapestry of unity.

But the true climax came when Malik, now a budding leader, organized a youth march. "We the Equal!" they chanted, signs blazing with equal signs. Jamal watched from the sidelines, Ms. Harmony at his side. "See? The arc continues."

As the sun set on that day, Jamal reflected on the illusion of equality. It was no longer a facade for him; it was a call to action. The Preamble's vision, without the pillars, crumbled—but with them, it soared.

And so, the story of We The Equal lived on, not in pages, but in people. Jamal Thompson, the boy who dreamed of balance, had become the man who built it—one signature, one conversation, one revolution at a time.

Yet We The Equal endures as a clarion call to all humanity: right the wrongs of the past and present by following the command of God to love one another.

We The Equal Merchandise can be found at the following URL: https://trueequity.creator-spring.com/